Letters from Lucifer

Beth,
Thanks for letting the light shine! God Bless,
Pastor Mike

MICHAEL C. STONE

Copyright © 2009 Michael C. Stone
All rights reserved.

ISBN: 1-4392-6536-4
ISBN-13: 9781439265369

DEDICATION:

To my dear wife, Laura, who is my right arm,
my rock, my angel, and my *Claudia*.

LETTERS FROM LUCIFER
...*Screwtape* Revisited

CONTENTS

ACKNOWLEDGMENTS vii

PREFACE ix

PROLOGUE xv

INTRODUCTION xvii

– DAMON BEFORE HELL'S REVIEW BOARD . . . xix

LETTER ONE: 1
NEITHER SEEN NOR HEARD: SATAN UNDERCOVER

LETTER TWO: 5
MEET THE CHURCH FAMILY

LETTER THREE: 9
A LONE VOICE IN THE WILDERNESS OF NOISE

LETTER FOUR: 15
LAW AND GOSPEL

LETTER FIVE: 23
THE SEARCH FOR CONSENSUS: A MORAL MAJORITY?

LETTER SIX: 27
SEX AND THE MARKETPLACE

LETTER SEVEN: 33
CREATING CHAOS: DIVISIONS IN THE CHURCH

LETTER EIGHT: 39
THE END: RAPTURE—GOING OR STAYING?

LETTER NINE: 43
COUNT IT ALL...WHAT?

LETTER TEN: 49
ANSWERED PRAYERS

LETTER ELEVEN: 53
WORSHIPING THEIR WORSHIP

LETTER TWELVE: 57
ANOTHER GIFT TO SPOIL: THE WORD

LETTER THIRTEEN: 63
PERCEPTION IS TRUTH...ISN'T IT?

LETTER FOURTEEN: 69
LOVE...AGAINST SUCH THERE IS NO LAW

ACKNOWLEDGMENTS:

This book was a collaboration of effort and editing for which I am so grateful. Thanks to Tish Dragonette Hargens, Louise Blood, Linda Williams, Bill Oelkers, Margie Oakes, and J.D. Wegner for their help in so many ways.

I hope and pray that this book will offer inspiration and encouragement for all of us to fight the good fight in this earthly battle, which though already won for us, is still ours to engage in this side of heaven.

PREFACE

The exhaustion and challenge I have felt after running four marathons does not even come close to what I felt in the writing of this book. On more then one occasion I was tempted to quit altogether. Writing from the devious perspective and mind of the Evil One is a grueling enterprise. It is no wonder that C.S Lewis in his writing of the *Screwtape Letters* used similar words to describe his experience.

It took a terrible tragedy that struck close to home to finally motivate me to finish this work. Recently a former neighbor and pastor of a large local church devastated his family and church family, by taking his life just before the first worship service. So what does that have to do with this book and my final motivation for its completion? I will let you connect the dots.

There are two premises behind this book; the first is that we do not give Old Scratch and his subtle workings nearly enough attention. If we did consider that our decisions and choices are not solely our own, it would impact our behavior. We might chose not to take that drink, pull that trigger, watch that movie, or not follow through with a myriad of other harmful actions. Knowing that we are not operating alone might be just the reminder we need to firmly stand against, rather than softly acquiesce to, life's temptations.

The second premise is that the best way for Old Scratch to truly bring down the largest number of victims is to start at the top—with leaders. If the leaders fall, from the political to the athletic, then their "followers" are likely to do the same or at least, to stand quietly and skeptically on the sidelines. Is anybody else noticing leaders falling in record numbers these days? Do we not hear over and over again "what next?" or "who next?" Does that not explain some of the palatable anger we seem to have which really questions the ability to trust any authority after having been burned by so many leaders? Is there anything that Satan could do to be more effective? Is it possible that he is sensing that the end is eminent, and he is turning up the heat?

If there was never a time in your life when a bad choice or decision may have been altered by a second thought to Satan's influence or if you cannot think of a previously respected leader who has fallen of late, then put this book down. It is not for you. If however, this makes some sense to you, then fasten your seat belts and read on.

The context for seeing Satan's undercover work is nothing less than a little fictitious church family- called Church in the Valley. Old Scratch can do his work in the church too. All of us are familiar with or have known of a church, large or small, that has had or is having internal tensions and divisions. I wonder what positive preventative or reconciliatory impact might be possible if there was even the slightest consideration that these conflicts might be playing into someone else's hand, and they might be fighting for the wrong team? As senior pastor of the largest church of my denomination in the southeastern United States, I was amazed that even with some 2,700 members, how just a few people could cause so much trouble and dissension for so many.

Looking back on this, I wish I had understood things then as I do now. In fact I will not judge those who made life particularly challenging for me then. How could I demonize people for their actions when I had not first called out the head of demons and pointed to his quiet but powerful role in these divisive actions that sought to stir things up and tear things down?   How differently would I have reacted if I had seen this early on? How differently might all these people have acted if *they* really knew that they were not acting alone, but that a silent third party was truly involved and had a vested interest in making things fail?

As a mainline-denomination pastor I rarely considered the possibility of Satan's involvement. I certainly never thought about Satan much as "a roaring lion ready to devour anyone or anything of God's." I believe my fundamentalist brothers and sisters often err by giving him too much power and influence and making him just the opposite of God. I could not abide by a simple understanding that if God was the one who helped them find a parking spot in a pinch, then it must be Satan who had prevented it. This approach makes Satan too simple, trivial, and blatantly obvious for me. But what if both of these approaches are wrong and exactly what he wants us to do. Either way makes too much or too little of what he is about. Both of these enable Old Scratch to do his real work and go easily unnoticed—not brought to light for who he is.

What if we were to consider all our choices in light of the involvement of this stealthy and unfriendly third party? What difference would it make in our lives if we considered that in everything from major choices to everyday decisions, this subtle, quiet one is trying to influence us? Whether it is an affair, a Ponzi scheme, watching pornographic material, cheating on our taxes, or tearing down someone it would give us all pause to consider that someone else might be influencing us to do such wrong.

What if our aversion to reading the Bible, or our fear of speaking in prayer to our best friend or our neglect of worship all had at the heart not just our own unilateral action but the subtle influence of another? What if our slander of another person was primarily motivated by someone else? Why do we randomly spend money and time on sporting events or entertainment but meticulously calculate the time in worship and resources we give to God? And why don't we question such glaringly obvious inconsistencies more often?

Why do the very people who read countless pages of *Harry Potter* and memorize *Dumb and Dumber* movie lines still have an absolute aversion to spending any time reading what these same people would call the Word of God? Perhaps someone else *is* influencing things here…and it's not us!

Is it possible that, by neglecting the possibility of his involvement in our lives, we have relinquished more control then we realize. Maybe we need to get the memo to see this world as a battlefield on which we need to engage, rather than just a playground to enjoy. But perhaps there is one who truly has great interest in us *not* reading that memo.

This book is a unique way of peeling back the hidden layers around us to truthfully look at ways Old Scratch might be doing his work in our world. Though we may not be giving him permission, we may also be leaving the front door unlocked and open. Unlike God, this one is not a gentleman who will wait to be invited in. Remember that the easiest way to lose a war is to never identify the presence of the enemy.

Welcome to the battlefield...

PROLOGUE

A recent conversation:

"Have you been wondering what the heck is going on lately?"

"Excuse me?"

"The world seems to be in such a mess. If people are not shooting each other with bullets, then they're doing it with words. If they're not cheating each other out of money, then it seems they're cheating on their spouses."

"That sure sounds negative, but I guess it may explain why I have been feeling so angry and out of control lately… almost violated."

"Yeah, this is very real. I mean who are we supposed to trust? Leaders have let us down. Political and religious leaders have cheated and lied to us, and business leaders have robbed us blind."

"I am angry! Why should we have to pay the price for someone else's sins."

"Sins? That's an interesting word—I haven't heard that used for quite awhile."

"But I guess just because we don't use the word much doesn't mean that it doesn't exist…does it?"

"That's for sure. The realities and consequences of sin, or whatever you want to call it, are painfully visible all around us."

"And I guess in us, too?"

"What do you mean?"

"Well, we all not only have the potential to do wrong, but we actually *do* wrong and harmful things to ourselves and to one another, don't we?"

"Yeah, but do you think it is *all* our doing? That we decide for ourselves to do such bad and destructive things? What if there is another influence outside of ourselves that tempts and encourages us in these things?"

"What do you mean like the devil or something?"

"Yes, I guess. You know just because we don't talk about him, doesn't mean he doesn't exist either...does it?"

"I guess you have a point. Maybe he likes to go incognito, under the radar, and undetected. I mean why *would* he want to be found out?"

"It *would* help me to know not just what but whom I am up against in this world."

"It might make all of us think twice about a lot of things that we were doing and saying if we thought there might be some outside force influencing our actions and words."

What would happen if..."

INTRODUCTION

Old Scratch, Lucifer, Satan—call him what you will— *is* alive and well today. What if C.S. Lewis's *Screwtape Letters* isn't just fun reading and interesting prose but actually gives us a glimpse into another dimension of reality. This reality tends to elude us in the normal course of a day, except for its by-products of destruction and brokenness witnessed all around us.

With the little Church in the Valley as the backdrop, this is an *inside look* at what Old Scratch can stir up, even in a seemingly *holy* setting. This sobering possibility may give pause and help leaders become aware of an uninvited and pernicious third party. May this serve as an inspiration for everyone to put on the full armor of God in this very real battle called life.

Satan is no respecter of institutions, organizations, persons, or families but is on the loose as a roaring lion, looking to devour whomever he can. In our time we are firsthand witnesses to an unprecedented number of leaders who have succumbed to some weakness or temptation and have lost their personal credibility and the loyalty of their followers.

The following situations give a brief glimpse of the "other side," from Satan's perspective, as he writes instructions to Damon, one of his demons. The increasing number of leaders who have been attacked and have fallen, makes one wonder if Old Scratch is realizing how late it is; intensifying his tactics, so he can take down as many as he can before his eventual demise and defeat. What is *very* clear is how unaware the Enemy's victims are of his work and presence. To mount a defense or counterattack, it does seem absolutely necessary to first acknowledge the enemy's existence. C.S. Lewis' concern, in his classic work the *Screwtape Letters* was that we might either make too much of Satan or too little. It seems that today we are more likely to do the latter. To ignore or to minimize the enemy is to guarantee defeat. The assumption in this book is that Satan, who is the father of lies and the great counterfeiter, is alive and working overtime in our world in many subtle and deceitful ways. How we live life changes dramatically if we acknowledge the involvement of this unwelcome third party. It serves us well to expose the darkness to the light and to reveal the offensive tactics of Satan. May this be an inspiration to draw even closer to our Good Shepherd, desiring from him and depending on him for the supernatural strength that he alone can give us in these latter days. May we all be blessed to finish strong and to hear those victorious words whispered in our ears as we cross the finish line of life, "well done, good and faithful servant."

DAMON BEFORE HELL'S REVIEW BOARD

"Damon, this is probably one of the worst days in my life, and I have seen some really bad days! It is my passionate desire to make others miserable, but I really, I mean *really*, do not like to feel this way myself!"

"We very seldom call meetings of the board such as this. In fact I can count the number of times we have done this on one talon! We have called you before this Review Board because you have failed your task miserably. That most recent worship service at Church in the Valley was an abomination and will create many problems for us for years to come!"

"As you recall, my concerns began early, when I had to call in reinforcements to cover your pointy little tail because of that Claudia. She is not only aware of our presence, but even worse, she knows so well the Enemy's presence in her life. She seems impenetrable, but your task is not impossible. Do not give up on her. You cannot give up on her. Especially with all the help you have been given! If you do not change your ways, there is a much hotter seat than the one you are in now reserved for you. If hate is not a strong enough inspiration for your action, then perhaps self-preservation will get you off your tail!"

"Damon, I am really going out on limb for you on this one. You see, there are even some demons who think you have switched sides! Your statistics would certainly indicate this. You have not made a single quota and have lost some to the Enemy who were once solidly ours. I am generally so fond of that word *lost*, but it pains me deeply to ever use it in reference to the Enemy. Damon, this is not some game we are playing! This has to do with eternal destinations! Remember, Damon, misery loves company, and trust me, I am planning on having as much company as possible. Need I remind you, since the Enemy is in control of time, so we must be diligent—always!"

"Damon, sit tight while we review a few of the letters I sent you about this congregation. Perhaps you misplaced or neglected to read them because you don't appear to have implemented many of my recommendations!"

"My first letter to you was straight out of chapter one of *The Purpose-Driven Demon's Manual*. The principle is the absolute commitment to invisibility: to operate completely undercover. Since you obviously did not read it before, I will read it to you now!"

"Damon, I hope that you realize that one of the reasons I am here with you in this review now is because, just as the Enemy never gives up in his attempts at redemption, so we can never tire in our business of condemnation."

"As stated in our manual, page twelve, section three C, 'The words *giving up* are not in our vocabulary, but rather are the outcome we desire for our hopeless victims.'"

Satan means accuser

LETTER ONE
NOT SEEN OR HEARD: SATAN UNDERCOVER

My Dear Damon,

This is just a strong reminder, an addendum if you will, to *The Purpose-Driven Demon's Manual*, which I trust you read eons ago, when you signed up for this job—or should I say *fell* into it? This is so essential to your mission that it bears repeating. It is absolutely imperative that you leave no visible footprints of your work to those on whom you are working. You must always be undercover. These humans need to go about the business of life without the slightest suspicion that there are any outside influences, and most particularly personal forces like us, that could have any sway over them at all.

They must always think that whatever choices and decisions they make are done fully by their own will and intention; that they are indeed total autonomous masters of their own fate. It is *absolutely* necessary that you realize that we are most effective when unrecognized or at most trivialized in cute phrases like the devil made me do it! They must perceive life as a playground of which they are in total control rather than a battlefield on which outside forces have constant influence upon them. Our success in ruining their lives is in large part measured by how much we run their lives, and how little they become actively engaged in this life. If there is no perceived enemy or battle, then there is no need to intentionally engage and make any conscientious, moral, or ethical decisions to counterattack or worse yet, to ask for help from our *real* Enemy? With people taking an attitude of such naive aloofness, you can make everything from church attendance, to Bible study, as nothing more than proud, pious acts to affirm one's righteousness; rather than acts of humble engagement against the likes of us. I much prefer their nice safe images of harps and robes than those of armor and spears—it makes our fight so much easier! You see, if there is no enemy like us to be considered, then such a battle need never be engaged, let alone fought. That is what makes it so easy to catch the most religious of folks off guard and then surprise the…shall I say …hell out of all those around, who cannot believe that such badness could come out of such good people. Never, I repeat *never* let anyone, even the victims themselves consider for a moment that they may have had some "assistance" in their fall. After all, we are pretty much experts when it comes to succumbing to a free fall.

Remember in all your work that a slow, deliberate, quiet, subtle manipulation works best. It is always beneficial to go undetected. This stealth approach will also be the hallmark of the Antichrist, so much so, that by the time he is recognized, he will have subtly worked his way into the hearts and minds of many.

Remember this is off the record—I didn't say it, and I'm not here.

Your stealth uncle,
Old Scratch

LETTER TWO
MEET THE FAMILY AT CHURCH IN THE VALLEY

"Damon, do you remember my letter to you some years ago about this church? I indicated even then that you had a unique opportunity to stir things up and make as much good go bad as possible. Let me refresh your memory as you seem to have forgotten so much!"
My dearest demon Damon,

    This church is like any other mid sized church, with all its blessings and challenges in a unique but typical bundle of humanity. The senior pastor, Tim Gilbert, is in his twelfth year of ministry at Church in the Valley. Maggie, his wife of thirty years, is a dear companion and helpmate. All three of their children are grown and have begun families and lives of their own. Damon, I do not believe that you have never used his relative success or title to appeal to his vanity like you could have.

    Then, there is that Claudia. She is a long-time member, and the first woman in this church's seventy-eight-year history to be elected council president. Damon, I still cannot believe you could not get some impossible-to-refuse male to tempt her into trouble. Although, I'll grant you, she is a tough one. She has unique qualities and already has moved too many to the Enemy's camp. Claudia pursues life with passion and is able to astutely articulate the most complex theological and philosophical concepts.

Mark is a recent convert and relatively new member at Church in the Valley. He has previously experimented with virtually everything one can imagine in life—from drugs to crime to sex. I recall one of the church members saying that "faith is the only thing up to this point Mark hasn't tried." Many of the church members were skeptical of his change and highly suspect of any longevity in this new addiction-free venture of his. Mark is resolutely holding on and has been able to let go of all sorts of addictions. Damon, whatever you do, don't let him fill that gnawing, void left by those chemicals with the Enemy's filling presence. And of course, encourage as much vocal cynicism from his many doubting skeptics as possible.

Next there is Oscar Lundgren. How easy has this guy been to work with? He is totally oblivious to our influence whatsoever. It has been a joy to have someone like this in different leadership positions within this church. Oscar is a third generation Valley member who can easily rattle off the date of his baptism and point out the pew that his family has laid claim to and darkened over the years. In his proud words, his family has "paid for our pew many times over." He has the self-appointed task, with his wife Ginger's strong bidding, to keep Pastor Tim straight on issues that the good pastor might otherwise erroneously assume he knows more about than Oscar. Such a help to us. If a vote were in the works on anything, and it looked to be unanimous, Oscar would feel most obliged to spoil it, asserting all the while that 100 percent in favor of anything just could not be good. I have full confidence that you can enlist his unsuspecting help in stirring up all kinds of "well-intended" controversy. We know all too well where good intentions can lead.

The Walkers are in charge of the greeting committee, and it would be impossible to pass through the front door of the Church in the Valley without being warmly greeted by these two. Mildred and Evan Walker ooze that despicable hospitality and warmth. Their poor stewardship of life can continue to work for us, as they are convinced that they need to spend every dime and minute on themselves before they leave this earth. They rather innocently make the poor envious and the generous confused. Help them in their spending addiction to continue "cramming for finals" anyway you can, Damon. Let them never give any meaningful consideration or desire to leaving a legacy behind of any more significance than some photo albums and shells.

As you know, Church in the Valley has grown over the years, but it has not kept up with surrounding churches, which are more progressive in their preaching and music styles. The recent hire of a young musician named Crystal to introduce new contemporary music to the church is a potentially great opportunity for us, of which you have only begun to maximize. Get the congregation so focused on the mechanics of worship that they forget *who* they are worshiping and why.

The fairly recent addition to the staff at Church in the Valley is the associate pastor, Brian Steffie. Brian is married to the beautiful young Sharon. The Steffies have three children, ages eight, five, and three. They have brought welcome energy to the church and have helped the younger generation to feel affirmed, as they can relate so easily to these young families and their life situations. You know Pastor Brian's weakness, and you have done a good job of helping to spread rumors and divide camps on the issue. His ongoing affair with Tiffany, the church secretary, has served our purposes well. I trust, Damon, that you will keep fanning that flame!

Song "I Belong" by Kathryn Scott - Claudia's song

LETTER THREE
A LONE VOICE IN THE WILDERNESS OF NOISE

"If you will recall Damon, the first of my many letters to you regarding this Claudia, I shared a poem that she wrote when she was only sixteen-years-old. I should have known back then that she would give you such a run for your money. I should have given you reinforcements early on … perhaps then she would not have won so many over to the Enemy's camp!"

Her poem: at age sixteen:

Be Still and Know
Surround sound,
Bombarded by
Chatter and clatter
Clamoring for attention
Unworthy
To open a soul

Or to lend an ear
If such verbiage
Of selfish agendas, political nuances
And subtle labels,
Were to be expunged
From all wavelengths
And exorcised from all sound.
Quiet
Would swallow up space
And empty noises would be filled with
Silence.
And in that hollowed but refreshing stillness
We would know
That then and only then
Is there room
To hear…
God."

"That was from my letter to you when she was but a late-blooming teenager."

My Dear Damon,

In this age of busyness and noise, you have sure let your Ms. Claudia seemingly escape from it all. How have you let her be so uninterested in the distracting noise of TV, iPods, cell phones, and computers? You know that silence, in a word, is…deadly. Have you not noticed that her quiet times with the Enemy are absolutely devastating to our cause? Is it not possible to distract her in those spiritual times? Surely, by now you have learned that if you cannot influence through

LETTER THREE - A LONE VOICE IN THE WILDERNESS OF NOISE

worldly distractions, you must create spiritual distortions. There must be some kind of way to spoil her special quiet times with the Enemy. Perhaps she harbors some smugness or spiritual pride with which you can tempt her. Try using some exclusive revelation—revealed only to her, to encourage a smug holiness about having these special times with the Enemy in the first place. Cloud her thoughts with judgment on all those "would-be" Christian, acquaintances who do not share her kind of disciplined devotion. Damon, do something, anything, but you must *do something*! Time and time again she comes empty and surrendered to the Enemy, and I for one, find it hard to believe that you have let her get this far!

You know, Damon, the Enemy created a restless hunger within the human spirit for more in this life. From the beginning, we have been able to direct this emptiness and craving for all the wrong things. Our goal and desire is for them to die hungry, never satisfied, and always searching in all the wrong places for satisfaction. Despite being so young, she has certainly seen past all your tricks. If she has nibbled on anything you have set before her to satisfy that hunger, she has been quick to spit it out and move on to a search for deeper meaning. She finds the vacuous emptiness of sin much like she finds the fullness and beauty of the creation—as things that point beyond themselves. How can you get her to commit idolatry if she is so insistent on worshiping not the objects but the Creator of these things? This is indeed a predicament we thankfully don't have to face very often. Everyone else seems to have soft places where they are easily tempted to get stuck. Who is this anyway—Joan of Arc? Is there no person or thing or object of desire you can set before her to get her off track? We are gifted, experienced, and very skilled at this! You must be able to find SOME all-consuming idol for her to fall down before.

I am afraid Damon that Ms. Claudia's peaceful satisfaction will be like a lighthouse and magnet of attraction to those around her. She is such an unmistakable contrast to those who are so hopelessly and aimlessly caught up in the hungering search for that which she has so quietly found. She has really come to understand that all she enjoys—from her pet dog, her love of art, music, and gardening, let alone her own sexuality, are but foretastes of something far greater and beyond. It is so difficult at this point when someone like her understands that all the joys and pleasures on this earth are but hors d'oeuvres compared to the smorgasbord on the other side. It is almost impossible to redirect someone like this. Continue to look for some crack, some interest, or some passion that she has not yet surrendered to the Enemy.

I carefully observed her the other day, noting that, even as she listened to Beethoven's Ninth or even that blasted contemporary Christian music, the focus of her affection is never on the object itself, but rather on the maker behind and beyond it. The art that she adores, the landscape she observes, and the gardens that she works in, do not claim her undivided attention. Instead, each inspires in her a keen interest in knowing fully the Creator of it all. I would never say give up on her, but I think I am running out of ideas. You might bargain with the Enemy to "sift her like wheat" with some tragedy or loss. Unfortunately with someone like this, such trials can actually make her faith stronger and her witness more devastatingly convincing to those around her, and then whole thing would backfire on us.

What about a tempting male, preferably a Christian who is more witty and physical than she? It is always nice to spoil two for the price of one, you know. I remember her fling with that young man years ago. But I recall that even that she turned into some "sacred awareness." Disgusting! How did she put it? "That the most cataclysmic orgasm on earth is but a handshake in heaven." That sent me howling in revulsion! I'm not sure that you can waste too much time on one like this. She is so far gone and so young. I think that you may have lost her. Unfortunately age will make this faith of hers more despicably sweet especially as it grows with time. Her demure, quiet faithfulness at such a young age is disgusting and makes her all the more dangerous for us. How about trying to make her equate her faith to an outward display of exuberance? At least she could join the ranks of those other obnoxious "odd-for-God" folks. Then those observing could easily write her off as another over-the-top fanatic. As it is, she is a tremendous liability to our cause as an incarnation of the Enemy's still calm voice in a noisy and desperate world. I fear that she will be very captivating and intriguing to those still looking to be satiated from the empty worldly helpings we eagerly place before them. At the very least, keep her away from as many humans as you can to minimize the damage!

Always and eternally hungering for more,
I am your starved,
Uncle Scratch

LETTER FOUR
LAW AND GOSPEL

"Damon, do you recall many years ago, when I wrote to you about Pastor Tim and how he was falling into the trap that so easily captures many of these religious types? He felt it necessary to clearly choose at all times between either Law *or* Gospel. You know the Enemy always kept the perfect balance between Law *and* Gospel. His dealings with the sinful woman at the Pharisee's home was one of many disgusting examples of how he held both the boundaries of truth and the graciousness of love together at the same time. So, here is what I wrote you..."

My Dear Damon,

Today your pastor *project* experienced a titillating moment of "righteousness" as Senior Pastor Tim passionately blasted some "outsiders" and then quickly expounded on a selection of scriptures "proving" that his disdainful view of these people was also shared by the Enemy. The response by a clear majority of those in attendance was, in my memory, one of the few instances in which the pastor was the beneficiary of such public affirmation. You are wise to capitalize on this need for acclaim, as his prowess in the pulpit has been sufficiently challenged by the new associate pastor, Brian. I would think that this exciting, spontaneous applause from his Bible class, in response to his pious pontifications, indicates that there will be many more attempts at mass appeal by him in the near future. Please, do whatever you can to feed this frenzy and this seemingly insatiable need. See if you can make the Bible study move away from the contents of the book and toward the opinions and views of the participants. You will know you have done this when everyone starts to feel smugly set apart. If you can, have them equate that exclusive righteous feeling with holiness; then you have truly succeeded. You must remember that the Crusades were waged on nothing more than blind passions like these.

You may be wondering what is at the root of these needs both for the pastor and for the parishioners involved. You evidenced the pastor's need both to be right and to be appreciated, which are essential ingredients of hubris. If this pride can be nurtured then "God knows" the potential for our work is endless. But besides this pathetic need by the reverend, there is also the need of these dear parishioners to have their religion delineated and spelled out clearly and cleanly, so that it can be served up in a palatable, tightly wrapped package. So you ask, what is the appeal for such neatness? Damon, you know that from the beginning of time there has always been a desire for a simple *religion* that clearly and neatly defines everything. Need I remind you that we much prefer this to an involved *relationship* with the Enemy, which has the complicated messy dynamics of faith and trust?

It is this desire for simplicity and clarity in religion on which you must capitalize. There have never been times as conducive to facilitating the need for black and white boundaries as these. The many undefined or gray areas within their pluralistic culture, give very few boundaries and even fewer, if any, absolutes. This creates a hunger for clearly spelled out lines determining right and wrong, as well as who is in and who is out. Many see this as the very definition of faith and the sole function of their religion. That is marvelous! Perpetuate that notion any way you can because there are many positive by-products if their religion is a well-defined, unbending, black-and-white boundary. The contrast to the rest of life helps creates that marvelous chasm between their experiences with God on Sunday morning, and the stark gray realities that await them on Monday morning in real life. Faith for them must be a system that provides a clear-cut, easily followed roadmap rather than a walk of trust into unknown territory. While you are at it, make them perceive the Bible as a religious rulebook rather than a relational love letter.

Damon, if you can get them into a very legalistic line of thinking, before long they will put their ultimate trust in their own particular religious interpretation, rather than in relationship with the Enemy himself. Encourage "faith" in their religious "prescription." Their brand of religion must take precedence over the person anytime. *Anytime* you can get their focus off Him and onto themselves and their particular system of beliefs, you have done well. You are not reinventing the wheel here. Like the Pharisees long ago, their system can be so self-sufficient that they won't even need the Enemy, let alone recognize him if he were right in their midst!

I call your attention to another aspect of this boundary creating that you must inspire at all times. Whenever a line is drawn in the sand, there will always be those who are in and those who are out. This delineation of outsiders must be clearly evident, since such radical exclusion is totally antithetical to the Enemy's way of thinking and acting. The use of language is extremely important here. Words such as *in, out, either,* and *or* are excellent choices to help the cause and create such boundaries. It is with great delight that you should help facilitate the pastor and his people's misuse of the Enemy's own words. And why not use some of his favorite words like *Law* or *Gospel*. Never let them use the article *and* between these words. Such a simple change can make all the difference in the world. A church then would be inclined toward one *or* the other. Put simply, a purely law-oriented church would emphasize who is in and who is out, and what one needs to do to get in. A purely Gospel-oriented approach would do quite the opposite, with absolutely no parameters whatsoever; this sort of church would have a theology that might be easily summarized in the words "everything is beautiful in its own way."

In a relational example, the one extreme is like a parent setting up boundaries to lay down the law for their children. It seems unthinkable that if these laws were broken, the child would forever be banished from the home and separated from the affection of his or her parents; it seems just as unthinkable that a parent would naively put up with any and all behavior from his or her child without consequences.

LETTER FOUR - LAW AND GOSPEL

In a home one would never act out either of these extremes, at the exclusion of the other, but this is exactly the kind of chaotic incongruity you are called to help foster within the church.

The Enemy often uses real life relationships and connections to convey truth, so please be sure to steer them away from any parabolic reality comparisons, as I have just shared, since they are quite damaging to our cause. Help them compartmentalize their "faith" as far away from the truthful relational realities of their everyday lives as you possibly can. The focus on scriptures must never dwell on relational situations, particularly of those involving Jesus, since he demonstrated perfectly that devastating balance of Law *and* Gospel in life. Consider his graciously sharing a meal with both prostitute and Pharisee, and how both left very different people than they had been before the meal. I shudder to think what a difference this little church and pastor could make, let alone the church at large, if they ever got this balance right. Whatever you do, make them feel that they need to do *either*, *or* not *and* when it comes to the Law *and* Gospel.

Oh, Damon, one last thing: besides confusing the Enemy's words, you might want to mess with his gifts to his children as well. You know by gifts, I mean the sacraments: namely baptism and communion. Make them fixated on questions like who is worthy to receive them, when do they get to receive them, and how do they get to receive them? Whatever you do make them focus on the *gifts* themselves and not on the *giver*. You can even make people within the same denomination squabble over correct mechanical or ecclesiastical techniques, or even the right spirituality necessary to receive this free, unconditional gift. And of course, the other side of the coin is to make the sharing of it so light and easy that it is perceived as an inconsequential symbol both to the recipient and those witnessing it.

In the same way, Damon, you can totally ruin this gift given for *all* people by making it exclusively for *some*. Make them try to figure out who is able to receive these *free* gifts by determining whatever label might somehow disqualify someone from this free, unconditional gift. I repeat, put righteous conditions on it at all costs, and then their focus will be on the gift and it's taking, rather than the giver and his sharing. You pick whatever label you can that will separate them and keep them from this table *of grace*. Damon, just a hint, those differences based most on perceived moral deviances seem to work better than those based on theological differences. The former gives the unspoken but palatable notion that only the "clean" and "perfected" can come to the table. An added bonus is that such a litmus test of the faithful puts undue pressure on the preacher turned policeman and then will no doubt go quite far in making parishioners much more critically focused on one another. Witchhunts within the church are truly hard to beat! Plus this puts the task of trying to transform lives on the *right people* doing their job, policing and protecting, rather than focusing on and worshiping the *right person* who has already done his job perfectly and completely for them.

In closing, Damon, keep it simple; just twist everything around, like key words and sacramental gifts. If you can turn what was given as a gift of love for *all* into an exclusive weapon for *some*, you can cause confusion and trouble beyond your imaginings. Now just think for a moment of the damage potential of those outside the church, silently and quietly watching and wondering if it is safe to come in. If you do this right, those outsiders will never risk so much as a step inside, and better yet, they will impute upon the Enemy the very ungracious exclusivity they have so painfully experienced from within the church.

Exclusively and Ambitiously Yours,
Uncle Scratch

LETTER FIVE
THE SEARCH FOR CONSENSUS: A MORAL MAJORITY?

"Damon, before I read this next letter to you, I am reminded of something that you never truly did get or use to your full advantage. These folks with their Sunday smiles want everyone to be happy and want everyone to agree and get along. Damon, there is no need to interfere with that nonsense, just cultivate that need to our advantage by creating inertia. You know, "an object at rest," - and we are all about inactivity. No movement is always good. So if you can get these nice people to do nothing, unless of course everyone is in full agreement on everything, then you've got it made! You recall my letter to you about Pastor Tim, don't you?"

My Dear Damon,

In your desire to thwart or stifle the efforts of the good Pastor Tim and his leadership, perhaps you need to learn a thing or two about using cultural presuppositions to your advantage. The one I find to be particularly insidious and damaging, for the cause of any good leader, is the need to always have consensus or majority opinion before any significant action or decision can be made.

The soft, warm, sweet desire for "niceness" in the church can even make such a perceived need for consensus the Christian thing to do! Prophets, who always stood alone, are not stoned today but are easily ignored as rude and inappropriate in their unilateral, unpopular stands. The information age, in which the pastor finds himself, encourages the desire for consensus, as the ability to check with the general public about any proposed change or new direction and is now the new moral imperative. Polls have not just become a tool to analyze popular sentiment but can be cleverly utilized by you, Damon, to stifle any forward progress. If you can convince those willing to listen, that absolute truth is relative and solely based on the majority whim of the day, on any given issue, at any given time, then think how many unpopular but good things you can prevent…even by a very narrow margin of victory.

One added benefit to this chaotic mass appealing is that you can convince those who have been given voice and vote that everything will go exactly as they had desired. Such a naive belief brings both a smile and a chuckle to me. Imagine the disappointment you can create! You could paralyze this leader from doing anything worthwhile short of putting a water fountain in the narthex hallway, and even that may still have a 49 percent dissent rating! If this majority rule becomes the rule of the day, as well as the expectation of the people, then you have effectively won. You can celebrate the victory on two fronts actually. First, you can prevent much of any consequence for the Enemy from being

LETTER FIVE - THE SEARCH FOR CONSENSUS: A MORAL MAJORITY?

accomplished, and second, in a most subtle way, you have made all who have "expressed" themselves feel that their opinion and vote is *all* that matters—the ultimate, and shall we say, absolute rule of authority.

Think, Damon, it was nothing more than two against one in the Garden of Eden—or was that three, including me against the one? We are so good at staying behind the scenes, aren't we? Convince them never to take the Enemy's voice into account, or better yet let them equate their voice to his. Imagine how little would have happened historically and how much evil would have prospered and prevailed today, if the majority would have *always* been needed before a leader could act. What havoc could have been wrought if the majority, "feel" for the day could have overruled any thought of an absolute truth?

If Moses had been subject to a vote of the people before presenting the Ten Commandments, imagine what would have been taken away or what amendments would have been insisted upon? Roosevelt certainly would not have entered World War II if consensus were his only dictate for action. How preposterous would it have been for Lincoln to have taken a poll on the relative merits of entering his nation into a civil war? Or consider their Lord pausing for a vote from the eleven on the night he was betrayed, as to the prudence of his going forward to the cross.

Never forget the example of Joshua and Caleb coming back from the Promised Land and being outvoted ten to two to move forward. What a marvelous dividend was found in this stalling of forward movement for the day, as they had to wander for forty years! Wandering is often a by-product of the majority always dictating direction. There were only two in that group asking, "What would God want us to do?" That is a question you must not let them ask, but rather encourage, "What do I want?" or "What do we need?" to be the questions which rule the day.

The immediate cozy feelings of satisfaction from expressing voice and vote, in determining their direction, can even be perceived to be well worth the long listless wanderings and lack of direction that follows. If you can convince both the shepherd and sheep that the only way to be effective is to always seek such overwhelming agreement, then you have in effect, paralyzed them. Remember that in their wilderness wanderings, Moses people consoled themselves those forty years with the knowledge that their voices were heard, and they did it their way. Never ever forget that the eternity of hell is passed by similar consolations.

Your undeniably, absolutely, overwhelmingly popular uncle,

Scratch

LETTER SIX
SEX AND THE MARKETPLACE

"Damon, now we are on to one of my favorite subjects, the attraction of the sexes. It is all about taking what was intended for such good and turning it into something so bad. It is all about disconnecting the fruit from the vine. Once disconnected, it is just a matter of time before this once healthy beautiful thing will start to rot. As I saw Pastor Brian hugging his wife this afternoon, I recall when it wasn't always like that. You did a good job of igniting his affair. Too bad you didn't finish the job. That Claudia certainly did not help the cause. The worship service several weeks ago, was a disaster the minute it turned into a confessional healing service. Damon, it is fine for them to talk about forgiveness and love, but whatever you do, at the very least, keep them as far away from expressing it and experiencing it as possible. Do you remember this letter? I wrote it when you really had Pastor Brian constrained on the very short leash of *I want and I need.*"

My Dear Damon,

    I hesitate to pat you on the back for I know firsthand the dangers of being puffed up. I have promoted that affliction so often to the detriment of many a victim. However, I must say you have of late done an excellent job of breaking up marriages and families, and destroying any sense of social stability, with this ever-present temptation of infidelity. With your help the new Pastor Brian has fueled the rumors into fact by his trysts with the church secretary. You have done a good job of blinding him to what he already has at home and moved him into new, uncharted territory with all the passion of a conquistador about to lay claim to a newly found land. Damon, my guess is that you simply tempted and encouraged him—probably not even recognizing what you were truly helping to facilitate. So let me unpack it for you.

We have for years promoted sexuality in so many different venues. It has always been wise to make even the most religious feel and appear prudish and out of touch. (No pun intended.) This heightened awareness and interest in the subject of sex has been a necessary foundation to make these many infidelities a reality. It was this exaggerated focus on sex that helped bring about this epidemic of unfaithfulness.

You see, Damon, it was this emphasis on sexuality, combined with the attitude of my right and need for it that truly clenched the deal. It excites me beyond description whenever we take anything that the Creator intended for good and even called it such, and twist it into something dirty and bad. The shame and fear of their first parents, as they frantically hunted for fig leaves to cover themselves, thrills me every time I think of it. The all-consuming emphasis on sex in TV, movies, and magazines has helped to make even the best

LETTER SIX - SEX AND THE MARKETPLACE

of people minimize its power and for all to be unsuspecting, benign prey to its captivating power.

The real tour de force in making all these good humans go bad—from preachers to teachers—was to move them from this marketplace mentality to the bedroom. Let me explain. Though you have seen this, perhaps you have not clearly understood it. In an affluent society the unabashed mantra is, "I want therefore I get." This heightened *want* can induce in the most sophisticated of adults a kind of whining angst to acquire or else, or as they often put it, "I cannot live without it!" This can be anything from a game, TV, car, or whatever you can lay claim to. For it is not the importance of the object—be it possession or person, as much as that all-consuming hunger to acquire. They can even give this passion for acquisition a religious fervor, saying that their lives, in the absence of this object of desire, will somehow be less than "what God intended for me." An insatiable hungering and grasping for possession rather than a respectful appreciation from afar is the goal, Damon! Although these fools cannot truly possess anything or anyone, but let them think that it is always their God-given right to do so!

The joy I get of blaming their sin on the sinless One is beyond description. This fervent desire to possess things is good—or should I say *bad*—enough? But if you can move that passion into the realm of possessing people, transforming them into commodities and objects of desire the potential is devastating! You cannot underestimate the overall power of such a move to wreak havoc and to dismantle the strongest of marriages, families, and respected institutions.

We have so skillfully and subtly removed from the marketplace any moral or ethical considerations, so that the only thought is the unquestionable and justifiable ultimate priority of self-interest. Just like my personal fall, the fixation on my will and my wants becomes its own ethic and morality, easily justified in the mind of the believer. If one need not give thought or regard to the poor, the hungry, or even to any process of purchase but ones self-interest, the move from possessions into the realm of people is such an easy, smooth, and slippery slope.

That is why, Damon, your subject, Rev. Brian Steffie, so easily and passionately rationalizes his affair with his secretary. He is known to think and say that this "special relationship" is his "right" and that even "God wants him to be happy…after all." Any ethical or moral considerations about such a passionate "purchase" in terms of the effects that will have on his wife and children, let alone his workplace, must succumb to this incessant very real *want*, which he would vehemently articulate as his very real *need*.

Damon, this whole process is so very slick and subtle that if it is promoted correctly, it can disconnect the perpetrator from the moral incongruities of his myopic decisions. The cries and tears of those hurt by his self-serving decisions must be drowned out by the relentless pleas of his own heart and soul for his own self-fulfilled satisfaction. A child's tantrum over a video game, that he absolutely must have, is a latent seed of the hoped for behavior to come of a sophisticated, self-centered adult. By debasing sexuality, we have made humans into property; always with the potential for acquisition.

LETTER SIX - SEX AND THE MARKETPLACE

Please, whatever you do, keep the tidal waves of blind selfishness moving forward. This very passion that drives people to stampede and trample others during sale day at the Mall is the same passionate drive that ultimately justifies such infidelities. But the added benefit, of involving people, in this is the potential to hurt and destroy innocent victims in its wake—particularly if you can bring down those who are considered leaders. REMEMBER THAT IT IS NOT JUST A DEBASED MORALITY, AS MUCH AS A DEBASED MENTALITY THAT NEEDS TO BE NURTURED IN THAT SIMPLE UNQUESTIONED FORMULA FROM INFANCY — I WANT, THEREFORE I GET. If that can continue justifiably unquestioned in the home by children and in the marketplace by consumers, then it is an easy jump into the bedroom by lovers.

It is, after all, my right and my *need* to be happy.

Yours discontentedly, disconnectedly—but passionately,
Uncle Scratch

LETTER SEVEN
CREATING CHAOS: DIVISIONS IN THE CHURCH

"With the good feelings that followed that worship service, the last thing they expect is someone like us trying to spoil their day. It is so easy to attack when nobody is looking, isn't it? Speaking of attack, do you remember the good old days when you had this church picking sides and fighting their own civil war? It was just plain inspiring…"

My Dear Damon,

    I found today's Bible study discussion, led by Pastor Brian, very interesting—especially when he talked about me…the devil. There seems to be a new fickle fascination with us and with our work. Historically, such interest has usually peaked when the chaos we are so adept at promoting was flourishing. The preoccupation with us is fine, as long as it perpetuates an unhealthy fascination or paralyzing fear. As you should know by now, anything that keeps the focus off the Enemy is to be encouraged and aggressively promoted, even if the focus is on us! It is, after all, rather flattering.

Do what you must to keep them focused on my familiar title as *the great deceiver* and not on what I do in bringing about deception and its ensuing chaos. Your dear Senior Pastor Tim is a great example. Continue to deceive him into thinking that he is here merely to serve and care for everyone else but is not worthy of any such personal care in return. Such self-deception, as you have found with the parishioner Mr. Lundgren, must be tailored specifically to each person. Mr. Lundgren does believe, quite in contrast to the "good" pastor, that the world truly revolves around him. His overly inflated ego is as wrong as the pastor's deflated ego. But you have done well in perpetuating their mutual deception, and I am delighted with the marvelous chaotic outcome. It is thrilling for us, and even for others around, to watch these two go at it. There are occasions when I think you could sell tickets to an unabashed public so desiring to watch these battles. This rather apathetic audience continues to promote this overt tension, rather than seeking any real truth or peaceful resolution. This silent applause and fascination of the infighting by the masses has always served us well in history. Mark Twain was right that these humans truly would rather attend a hanging than a book signing. Let such misplaced fascination never be questioned, but continually nurture the feeding frenzy.

What began as simple butting of heads between these two people, in this equally shared deception of personal glory and personal sacrifice, has now festered and rippled out into the entire community. Any deception left unchecked will always extend into the unnamed, often misunderstood by-product-chaos. There will be those who are not so intrigued

LETTER SEVEN - CREATING CHAOS: DIVISIONS IN THE CHURCH

and fascinated by this active tension, and who, actually desire to get to the bottom of this conflict. Please do your best to stifle any move toward resolution; encourage instead everyone to choose a side, as they buy into either of these respective deceptions. Take particular care that the pastor and parishioner never have an opportunity to relent or repent (how I despise that word) from their strongly held positions. Do not let the pastor even think of things like joy and self-fulfillment as desirable or designed by-products of his relationship with the Enemy. And keep Mr. Lundgren and his ever-expanding gang as far away from humility as possible. Ensure that he has a well-fed and outsized ego. Both men will have the marvelous self-deception of being sacrificial martyrs for their respective causes.

Damon, please understand this truth about deceit: chaos will flourish when unchecked deceit takes root. *Any* introspection, particularly about the cause of the chaos itself, is to be kept to a minimum. Unfortunately, the Enemy often uses such friction as an opportunity for people to question and reflect. Even the most depraved and deceitful person might make use of such opportunity as this. So keep everyone as "healthy" and as focused on their "righteous" positions as possible, and they shall be more deeply entrenched than ever. Remember, there is a battle going on; don't picture white flags but foxholes, with everyone digging in deeper and never retreating or surrendering. *Surrender* is another word that makes me shudder!

I hope that by now, Damon, it is clear that the desired dividend of this fighting is to divide the church. I have countless such trophies to my credit! Churches have split, and the respective teams have suited up year after year to do battle for no other reason than to justify actions and to jockey for their relative imagined position. If the simple, trivial causes behind such splits were ever revealed, it would truly be embarrassing and evident that some other force (like us) must have also been at work. Be aware that the Enemy, namely the Holy Spirit, is particularly active at any chaotic time like this, looking for a crack in the self-righteous armor through which he can seep in. Once the Spirit begins to come into these soft and broken places, it is *very* difficult to reverse the process. This Spirit has a way of bringing the light of truth to this dark illusion, and reversing and softening all that hardness you have worked so diligently to create. The spirit makes one see personal sin and brokenness, which brings with it the desire for forgiveness and repentance. It makes me nauseous to even consider such things as these.

Damon, I reiterate that you must work feverishly to never let there be a break in this armor, lest all your work be for naught. This Spirit can grab a foothold, particularly if the leaders have some personal crisis, like death or illness, which causes them to pause or reflect. Those are both dangerous words as they give opportunity for change or repentance. Never, I repeat *never*, let that happen. Each person has their own reason not to pause or reflect. For Mr. Lundgren, it has been his own inflated sense of self-importance that would never allow the luxury of such idle time. For the dear Pastor Tim, he cannot afford to stop his important busyness, preoccupied as he is with caring for others; luckily for us, he is comforted by the knowledge that the Enemy will provide him the supernatural strength to do so. Keep the reverend

LETTER SEVEN - CREATING CHAOS: DIVISIONS IN THE CHURCH

away from any scriptures that remind him of his Lord faithfully taking time away for prayerful reflection. Maybe the pastor's Lord needed such reflective quiet times on earth but keep the pastor convinced that he has no such need himself!

You see, Damon, if you can keep those simple folks from retreating or stopping to look back at all, you have succeeded. Never give them time to reflect on the gods who deceive them now and have failed them in the past. Keep them so busy grabbing for the next worthy project or program to come along that they fail to notice the rubble or dust of shattered idols and dreams left behind. If they build today on the unresolved, failures of a broken past, you can then ensure a shaky foundation in the future. Damon your work now guarantees a legacy of trouble to come, and it is never a bad idea to prepare today for job security tomorrow.

Your rabble-rousing relation,
Uncle Scratch

LETTER EIGHT
THE END: RAPTURE— GOING OR STAYING?

"Damon, perhaps one of our best attacks is to get our victims entrenched in the things of this world. Wasn't it just a week ago they had a funeral here? You might think a funeral to be the last place in the world you could promote this world! But think about how many of them were grateful that they were not in *that* box. So you must be much craftier than you have been. After all these thousands of years, I really shouldn't need to tutor you so much! But think! Let their minds wander as to why they are glad they are not in the deceased's place. Think of the many ways you can remind them of all the earthly goodies—even people—that they would hate to give up. Regardless of how approvingly they nod their heads at all the sermon dribble about this not being their home, make this their home! Make it as comfortable and as welcoming and enticing a place as you can. Remember to do what ever you must to keep them focused on the here and now; on this time and this place. If you do a good job of this, they will be convinced that this is their only and final home!"

My Dear Damon,

Recently there has been, among the Enemy's people, an increased focus on the end of time, particularly in their fascination with the Rapture. For a word that never appears in their Book, there certainly are many "experts" who seem to know all the details of the end. This overly confident fixation should be nurtured by every means possible. This desire to have "control" and to know the future reminds me of the garden, and their first parents' urgent desire for knowledge and control, which of course started this whole mess.

Their Lord candidly admitted on earth that he did not know the time or details of the end but his Father did. When you can accelerate the need for such knowledge, you have helped to substitute power and control for faith and trust, and that is always good.

The desire to be "taken up by their Lord" at the Rapture is interesting. This is at best a religious fervor that you could easily reverse. The best way to keep them from wanting to leave is to make this world as enticing as possible. Do what you must to make this "foreign land" as cozy and as much a home as it can be. The more enamored with this world they can be, the less likely they will be ready to leave for the next. Lot's wife and her staunch refusal to leave home is one of our great trophies. Though fondly looking back on this world, at the Rapture, will not turn one into salt, it may make one lose his or her single opportunity to leave this place. I know the Enemy well enough to know that he is always a gentleman. We eagerly force ourselves on anyone and everyone at every opportunity, but this One never goes into places he is not invited nor entices people to go places against their will.

LETTER EIGHT - THE END: RAPTURE—GOING OR STAYING?

Remember Eden. The first ones could not stand to stay in that perfect, beautiful garden but had to go find greener pastures. He did not prevent their freedom of choice. What about the Israelites wandering in the wilderness and desiring to go back home to Egypt? Think about it: they wanted the familiarity of slavery, with its three meals a day, rather than the unknown Promised Land. Damon, the promised land of heaven must be seen as such a frightening prospect compared to the familiar green pastures of home. Our best work is to make this world so comfortable and so endearing that no one would want to leave it. My guess is that the Enemy, ever the gentleman, will oblige and leave those behind who would rather stay. Make this world as close to the enticing Babylon as possible. Most would rather stay with the seen fragrant hanging gardens here, than go to some promised unseen garden in the hereafter.

You see, Damon, the more you get these people rooted and connected to this world, the harder it will be for them to let go and be uprooted to the next. When the Enemy Spirit creates that horrific restlessness and longing for something more than this world can offer, you must work quickly to quench that yearning hunger with all the satisfactions that this world can possibly provide. In the past, the Enemy has never forced even the closest ones against their will. Damon, you, however, must use as much influence on their will as you can. Don't forget that as long as they are here on this earth, they are playing on our turf and hopefully our game!

Here for the long haul and sold out on this world,
Uncle Scratch

LETTER NINE
COUNT IT ALL...WHAT?

"Feelings are such a nice thing for us to manipulate any way that we can. Like sex, these feelings are part of the Enemy's arsenal, and he uses them to further solidify and nurture relationships. We do well in both of these areas to overemphasize their importance. Take Mr. Lundgren or Mark, for instance…please! Utilize their eager expectation of a 'good' warm feeling to come on them in this worship service. If we can get them to totally equate these good feelings with faith, we have it made. Because you see, when they step out the door into the rough-and-tumble world, and these feelings quickly dissipate, they will have to assume that they have no faith or better yet, no God. That brings up a sore point for me, Damon—Mark. He was so far gone, actually living in our domain on earth, and you let that Claudia get a hold of him and introduce him to the Enemy.

Do you recall that service several weeks ago, when Mark finally totally surrendered to the Enemy? Such a hideous sound when the Enemy's heavenly chorus broke loose in song and laughter. With my good instruction, you should have done better with Mark, and after this meeting you had better! Remember my words to you years ago?"

My Dear Damon,

Your latest experiment, with the new convert Mark, is truly a challenge. Just as the Enemy surrounds a hard heart with his Spirit, waiting for a crack, so he may seep in, so you must surround this newly softened heart. You must wait for some outbreak of hardness with which you can pierce through with some temptation or doubt. Timing and aim is everything in this process. Mark believes that he has found the Enemy, and, unfortunately, that the Enemy has found him. That combination is deadly. It is much easier if the *would-be* believer focuses solely on their finding the Enemy. You see, Damon, if all the *finding* of the Enemy is up to the believer, then so is all the losing, and then faith can be a very fickle venture. I do so enjoy that aspect of it. But, it becomes a problem when the Enemy's action is given credence in this faith venture because, as we know all too well, the Enemy is never fickle. He never gives up or loses anyone! Some would say that the playing out of history is His waiting for me, yours truly, "the lost sheep," to come home again. Flattering, but I am not buying it! Please do what you can to get Mark's focus on himself and his own faithfulness not on the Enemy's faithfulness to him.

This Mark we know very well, from all of his abusive childhood relationships. Throughout his life we have maximized this lack of trust for virtually anyone. You see, Damon, if he cannot trust someone who can be seen, it is such as easy task to keep him from trusting in the unseen presence of the Enemy. We have done a marvelous job of keeping him completely numb, up to this point, with his many addictions to drugs and sex. These have provided heartache and disenchantment for those around him and provided an escape for him from an untrustworthy world. His rationale for such destructive behavior has been logical and predictable. Now he is perpetuating the cycle of destructiveness of which he was a victim in the past, but now he is his own victim. It is one of those strange human phenomena—when they prefer controlled, predictable self-inflicted destructive behavior rather then the unpredictable, random cruelty that this world so often inflicts upon them.

So, Damon, how and when did you let him relinquish control? How did you ever for a moment let the notion of surrender and trust even cross his puny mind? To even let his path cross Claudia's was your first mistake! Claudia is very dangerous to our cause. Not only does her outside physical attractiveness capture instant attention, but her inner beauty and charm makes the most controlled male apologetically contrite for missing her true strength. Whatever you do, isolate her! Her work with Mark in rehab was devastating. She has that quiet prayerful way that reeks of the Enemy and oozes his compassion. It is such a gooey, sticky mess! Mark fell in love with her and then she gently invited him to fall in love with the Enemy. She even convinced him that the Enemy was trustworthy.

Her consistent and constant attention to him; something he had never experienced before in this life, did not help. This Claudia seems to mimic too well the Enemy's consistency of words and actions. With her invitations to church,

I was at least hopeful that Mark might be disconnected and disenchanted or at the very least, dismissed by the people that were there. Unfortunately none of that happened and that blasted Pastor Tim actually got to Mark through his sermon.

As you recall, Pastor Tim had everyone's attention as he spoke about his experience as a chaplain at the Catholic Hospital. He shared that every room had a crucifix hung on the wall at the end of each bed. As with all church symbols, this one has no power when devoid of any relational experience, but Pastor Tim shared that when he prayed with a woman, she shared her difficult story. She shared about her children leaving her alone, her divorce, and her terminal illness, which would soon claim her life. Pastor Tim shared that he did not know what to say to her. It was then that she pointed to the crucifix on the wall, and in tears she said, "At least I know that he is with me." There was not a dry eye in the sanctuary, and unfortunately Mark's hard heart softened at those words. For the first time in his wretched life, he realized that regardless of how alone he had felt before, in his pain and hurt, the Enemy had always been with him.

You are best to not even try to intervene in those moments, as they are beyond our means and power. It would be easier to take a rowboat upstream against Niagara Falls then to try to be effective in those moments. So do not waste your energy; there will be other opportunities. Remember always, that the timing of what you do is so crucial. Try to do what you must to get him past this "feeling" of closeness to the Enemy. As far as Mark goes, it is imperative that you make him crave these feelings of comfort and compassion so much that he ends up equating his faith and his ability to trust the Enemy with those "religious" feelings. In fact, for a short while, do whatever you must to make his new life as comfortable as possible since you want him to ultimately believe in this new "feel" rather than in this new relationship with the Enemy.

As I shared earlier, wait for the right timing to let loose the arrows to pierce his fragile heart during difficult times to come. He will most conveniently doubt his faith, if he has completely equated a lack of troubles and doubts with his new faith. We must always promote the idea that faith is equal to and dependent upon favorable circumstances. This works particularly well with someone like Mark, who has had so many disappointments in relationships. Let the Enemy and his followers be one more big disappointment in Marks' life. Make the Enemy seem either too uninterested or ineffective in making good the bad times.

Never let him consider that his faith in the Enemy is independent of any unpleasant or challenging circumstances but that such difficulties could actually sharpen his untried faith. By the way, with regard to Claudia, she continues to be a pesky bad influence on Mark, with her display of such unconditional commitment to him and to the Enemy.

Your finding fickle followers for a feeling-based faith
I feel good…or nothing at all,
Uncle Scratch

LETTER TEN
ANSWERED PRAYERS

"Damon, the only thing that gets less attention and mention than *us* is this thing called prayer. Just consider how little they talk about prayer! If they only knew its power and how many of them are here right now because of Claudia's prayer for them—yes, silence is golden on this one!

Do what you can to muzzle their talk about prayer and, of course, most importantly do what you can to prevent them from praying. This is right out of our manual!"

Dear Damon,

Without a doubt (oh! how I love that word), the most damaging and far-reaching threat to our work that you will ever face is that of real and genuine prayer. I mean honest communication before the Enemy that speaks straight from the heart. The kind of prayer that young Pastor Brian prayed with his wife as they both knelt, and he confessed again his infidelities before her and the Enemy. His tears were real and pathetic with the kind of sweet sincerity that makes me want to vomit. It is that kind of emptied, contrite heart that seems to get the undivided attention of the Enemy.

So Damon, whatever you can do to get the would-be prayer distracted from this disturbing habit the better. At the very least, let them think that prayer is all about them and that it can be done in a casual, disconnected way. Encourage the rhythmic and rote repetition of sayings like 'God is great, God is good, let us thank him for"... because making them so simple is a marvelous way to minimize the power of prayer. Let them never think that the Enemy wants or desires a deeper conversation with them. The more this can be a one-way, meaningless communication sent heavenward, the less likely there will be any expectations of earthbound answers in return. As much as possible, have them consider prayer to be a pious monologue with little expectation of response. I cannot help but chuckle thinking about how such apathetic, detached conversations as these would go over with a spouse. Never let them realize that the Enemy desires more interactive communication, just as in any other healthy relationship.

Jesus' insistence on addressing the Enemy as Father, or worse yet Daddy, is a horrific invitation to personal communication, which you truly must resist on all levels. With the likes of Claudia, who has this prayer thing right, you must convince her that there are so many more important activities that she could be about than prayer. Claudia is in a kind of constant communication with the Enemy; she will quietly engage in everything from thanking Him for a butterfly perched on her windowsill, to asking for help for an obviously distraught waitress, to lifting up concerns as they are brought to her mind about people far removed in the past or many miles away. There must be some way to discredit this woman's credibility, if not sanity, so that her audience and influence might be lessened.

Her prayers for this new convert Mark, has the Enemy building an impenetrable fortress of His presence around him. She must never know the powerful, unseen—but very real—spiritual power behind her prayers. If you can minimize the perceived power behind prayer, you will have greatly reduced the chance of any meaningful engagement in it. With her persistent incarnate-like involvement with those for whom she prays, it is no wonder the Enemy listens to her! She does not take this prayer lightly nor does she expect that every thing she asks for will be the answer given by the Enemy.

Damon, she understands far too well the posture of prayer as exemplified by the Enemy in the garden, when he asked that the Enemy's will to be done over and against his own. She also gets what so few of these naïve believers can't quite get—if healing was all that was needed or if life was always the answer, the Enemy would certainly give it.

The multiplying affect of prayer is our greatest threat. One person like this, armed with just a few prayers, can call forth the needed resources of a whole legion of demons like you to counterattack. Damon, Claudia is more than you can handle by yourself, so I am sending reinforcements immediately!

I shudder to think of her starting a prayer group at the church. You must at least have them talk about prayer more than they engage in it; bumping the gums is always more important than bending the knees! If a prayer group starts, you can work on the other members. Let them be so enamored by and caught up with Claudia's spirituality and connection to the Enemy that they are like a doting fan club, more interested in mimicking her technique than personally communicating with the Enemy.

Always interested in facilitating an empty, simple, trite, one-way monologue…called prayer.

Your prayer exterminator,
Uncle Scratch

LETTER ELEVEN
WORSHIPING THEIR WORSHIP

"Worship at its worst...or should I say *best*, must always have that hunger and craving to be fed and taken care of. The worshiper must be an expectant spectator waiting to see how they will be inspired or entertained or (how I love these words) asking 'if they get anything out of' the experience. It is quite the opposite of what their worship is supposed to be and often has the great side effect of leaving them hungering for the experience they craved but think they missed. Damon, it is so easy to promote that marvelous church *hopping* and *shopping* to find the right 'feel' when such selfish searching is the primary goal."

My dear Damon,

You have learned by now that the best time to turn up the heat in a victim's life is the very time when the heat of life is already searing. Vulnerabilities and weakness should always be exposed and kindled until the desired result of an out-of-control wildfire is reached. Now Damon, is the time to really start working on Pastor Tim. At forty seven years-old and with twelve years at this church, he is vulnerable when it comes to his self-identity. It is at those marvelous junctures, such as midlife, that you can most easily expose and prey on these humans' weaknesses. Since possessions are not really part of Pastor Tim's repertoire of needs, a new sports car or an affair, are probably not likely diversions of choice. Pastor Tim, as you know, has a great desire to please. In fact, part of his piety is his desire to please others more than himself. He even equates success with what others think about him. His current need is fulfilled by the recent hiring of Crystal, the young, sharp, energetic music director.

His desire to do something new and better stems from his participation in the recent Super Church Conference. He and thousands of others paid good money to hear enthusiastic, informed, and successful speakers tell them what they were not doing right and how they could do it better. Did you not notice how he returned after the conference with this tail between his legs? He was informed that *his* church was not measuring up in growth and numbers. If you'll remember, it was after this conference that he hired Crystal, thinking that all her creative and innovative ideas might move the Church in the Valley to the next level?

Keep Pastor Tim fixated on reaching his own next level. Just perpetuate his total dissatisfaction with the level at which he finds himself—and it will eat away at him. The Enemy could care less about such man-made levels, but let the good Pastor continue to feed this nefarious goal of numbers and forward momentum. Let him forget the Enemy's preoccupation with purposeful, one-on-one personal discipleship. Rather than deliberately moving forward and seeking the Enemy's directions, the good pastor must be inspired to charge forward first and ask for spiritual endorsement of his plan later. The carnage that can be left behind in such a stampede, in the name of growth, can never be taken lightly. Move him further and further away from the individual personal touch, which so excites the Enemy. Let success be measured solely in size, dollars, and numbers—not by changed lives, care, and compassion.

You see, Damon, the public accolades the pastor will receive in this new mission will help assuage his need for pleasing the crowds. The most specific task in this plan is to center around the worship experience. Those from Church in the Valley who attended the conference workshop service all asked why can't that be done here? Crystal is Pastor Tim's answer to that question. Set up, as quickly as possible, the entire agenda for worship to be all about them. Make them preoccupied with technical, practical questions like how effective it is, how everyone felt when they left, and whether things like sounds, lights, music, and message were "professional." This kind of preoccupation with such details will actually enable deep dissatisfaction, as no one will get *all* that they want. It will definitely keep the good pastor up late at night wondering who really is happy about all the changes after all. In the middle of all these changes keep their focus off spiritual concerns and what the Enemy desires in worship. They might be surprised and disappointed to know how little of what they find to be essential, the Enemy would even consider truly necessary for worship.

Damon, if you have not noticed, and I am concerned about all that you *do* miss, the good pastor is also very concerned about his preaching. Pastor Brian, who is both new to the church and younger than Pastor Tim, does not use notes at all and paces around in a most engaged and energetic way as he preaches. This made Pastor Tim take notice and made him more than a little envious. You know what to do with this envy. Unchecked, this worthy emotion can evoke all kinds of helpful responses to our cause. If you can get this envy within the context of worship, you can create a kind of perpetual hungering, which can starve any possibilities for truly Enemy-focused worship.

Keep stoking all these fires, so they burn as brightly as they can. And make the pastor and staff assume that the only audience they are accountable to and need to please, are sitting in the pews. Never let them consider the true *Audience of One* who has called them together to worship in the first place. If you can get them to focus on the event and worshiping their worship, they will miss the Person every time.

Worshiping everything but…Him
Your worship worthy,
Uncle Scratch

LETTER TWELVE
ANOTHER GIFT TO SPOIL— THE WORD

"Damon it is still amazing to me, even after all these millennia, that these mortals do not need much assistance to get themselves off track. It is not enough to consider retiring, but if we merely leave these earthlings to their own devices, they are very good (or should I say *bad*?) at neglecting the tools of the Enemy. I mean things like prayer and the Word. At the very least you would think they might ask themselves why they have such an aversion to opening or even holding that book. If they think he is listening, why are they not speaking up more? And if they think the Bible is his Word to them, why is everything else so much easier to read? They really don't see our part in this, do they? That means we are doing our job well. Never let them seriously consider these questions. Do what you must to keep them out of that Word. Even use "good" people, presuming they are doing "good," to keep "good" folks out of the good book. You will never regret it."

My Dear Damon,

Young Pastor Brian is proving to be excellent material for one of the oldest tricks in our book...namely to get attention off of the book. It is something that dates back to the Enemy's earliest followers who we enticed by a group called the Gnostics. These were supposed believers who had hidden or secret knowledge of and insight into the Enemy. From their very beginning, these simple humans have had an unrelenting obsession with uncovering any secret or previously *unknown* knowledge. What other tree could have been as tempting...as the tree of knowledge? For the life of me I do not understand this human need, but I do know that these "special ones" with such unique, previously unknown knowledge have a power that can make others green with envy. In recent times, we have used secular publications to satisfy this inner hunger for "new" findings or insights. The obvious positive by-product is that it keeps their focus and attention off the known Word.

This desire for such special knowledge can be used in all kinds of creative ways. Since Pastor Brian is so young and fresh from the seminary, it is expected by all, including his boss, Pastor Tim, that he has both the newest and most relevant of insights. You have done well to let this power of knowledge go to his head, particularly since parishioners concede to his educated insights about the scriptures.

It was amazing that no parishioner even flinched when he single-handedly refused to allow a group from another church group to use their building for Bible study on the grounds that the bible study material was "theologically incorrect." Oh, the mileage we have gotten out of those two words over the years! To be *theologically correct* separates these *elite* at an advantage to all the *plebeians* who know no difference and care not to invest the energy to find out. Whether it was the first century, the sixteenth century, or any church today, the subtle but meaningful equation of, (knowledge = power) should always be used to our advantage; most directly by keeping the "simple folk" out of the Word in the first place! This desire for such superior knowledge is no respecter of denominations. In fact, do not let Pastor Brian see the inconsistent hypocrisy of his dismissing this one group from using his facility for Bible study when today he was so upset when the tables were turned on him. He tried to get the new best seller from a Christian bookstore and was promptly told that they did not sell it because it was "doctrinally incorrect," though they would sell it if he would sign a disclaimer, getting them off the hook for any "theological misdirection."

He was quite upset with this, as he had no problem with that book. But he never once considered that the same rationale that prevented the store from selling him the book was the same that kept his church doors closed to an outside Bible study group. The ultimate and very convenient result of such nonsense is not just the disenchantment of those cut off, but also the ultimate good of just keeping people out of the Word entirely! The more those on the outside can find that *only* those on the inside know how to read and interpret the Word, the easier our job is! Let those elite educated religious folk feel that they must be consumed with helping the Enemy any way that they can, so that the Word is dispensed and interpreted correctly. Never let them consider that the Enemy might be big enough for the task. And do not let them ever consider the promise that the Word would not return void even without the caveats of any special interpretation to help in the process.

Throughout the ages, there have been such "helpers" for God, who interpret the Word and attempt to make it more palatable or clear in defining what the Enemy meant to say. Bibles have been rewritten, removing the slightest reference to the supernatural, questioning whether God has the power to do such things. Recently we have had a resurgence of the first-century Marcion in the removal of those things from the Word that God obviously did not intend to say or do. The Enemy is not too fond of this, but Damon, in situations like this, we should help in any way we can. Words such as *sacrifice*, *war*, *blood*, and *jealousy* are all out. With the most reverential flip of a pen or press of a key, you can make God irrelevant to any of life's difficult challenges.

This latest attempt at speaking for God by rewriting what *He meant to say* is nothing new, but oh so helpful to our cause. Damon, you will see that the sweeter and more comfortable they can make this Word, the better. For the less connected the Word becomes to the real harsh realities of life, which is not always so sweet, the less impact it will have on real life. If all reference to the troubles and complexities they experience in this life are removed from the Word, then you have helped remove and certainly minimize its relevance to *real* life. We are all about that, Damon! The power of this Word of theirs is precisely in its straightforward, honest, and uncompromising look at life. If you can eliminate such language as the "valley of the shadow of death," then when this valley is experienced in real life, they certainly would not expect the Enemy's presence with them!

So keep the religious ones sparring over theological correctness and doctrinal purity, while the secular ones attempt to rewrite what God meant to say. All in all, the goal is the same, and both are most helpful. The more you keep them away from the Word and the less relevant you can make it to real life, the more distance we can create between its Author and them.

Your…let me change it to what he *really* meant to say,
Special-knowledge dispensing,
Uncle Scratch

LETTER THIRTEEN
PERCEPTION IS TRUTH...ISN'T IT?

"This worship service is one which I will not soon forget, as hard as I might try to do so! Some of the run-at-the-mouth humans whom you rather craftily inspired to start the rumor mills about Claudia and Mark stood up to share and ask for forgiveness for what they did. I *cannot* endure another service like *that*! Those who questioned Claudia's leadership motives have also confessed to doing wrong. Damon, I think every bad thing you set in motion in this place has been turned around. You should know by now that you can never rest on your briars! There is *always* work to do! Never forget that the Enemy never rests and has a deep, relentless compassion that we will never understand or be able to match. So, even as I share this with you there are opportunities slipping by. I hope this letter sounds very familiar..."

My devious Damon,

It is admirable that as of late you have been taking advantage of the cultural phenomenon that equates perception with the truth. A person's public persona has now replaced his or her private realities in terms of societal importance. One could say that success truly is to fool most of the people most of the time. The importance of polls certainly reiterates this point. Critiques of leaders are totally centered on how they are coming across, not on what they say or do or the truth within.

This incongruity is not only enabled by, but also celebrated and capitalized on by the media. They will, on the one hand, produce movies and TV programs that openly glamorize infidelity and any lack of morality. Yet they are the first to use vindictive criticisms to expose any public figure who caved in to the very immorality they had simultaneously promoted. Duplicity and inconsistencies such as these are at the very heart of hypocrisy and help to foster the constant tension between one's public and private life. What one does behind closed doors matters little, if at all, if one is not found out. Public perception is the ultimate goal and final truth. The new right and truth is how one is perceived, and the new wrong and loss is getting caught or exposed. This kind of incongruity and hypocrisy needs to be fostered on every level of leadership from politicians, sports figures, CEOs, presidents, pastors, and all leaders. All are susceptible to this cultural misconception that their accountability is not to an absolute truth or to the Enemy but rather to satisfying the public they are supposedly serving and leading. This has served our cause well from the White House to the church house, where we have made the question, "How am I coming across?" more important than, "Am I doing the right thing?"

LETTER THIRTEEN - PERCEPTION IS TRUTH...ISN'T IT?

This marvelous obsession with public appearance and perception has been around forever. Consider the Pharisees, whom the Enemy so aptly described as being like whitewashed tombs on the outside but containing dead men's bones on the inside. Inside and outside inconsistency is truly living in that dichotomy between one's public and private life. The difference between then and now is that, with the help of the media, you can help exaggerate the importance of the public appearance. Damon, some of the Enemy's most effective men and women in history would not stand a chance in today's public-appearance-driven world. Public appearance means even more than substituting words and actions. It now involves spin, appearance, and persona. We have used this to our advantage time and time again. You see, today, the most simple but "presentable" Saul stands a greater chance of being chosen as a leader than the most gifted David.

Damon, this priority of cultural appearance can be used in every organization imaginable. Public opinion can be used to promote as well as tear down a potential leader. If you are wise Damon, you will use this to your advantage. Recall our involvement with the Enemy when Jesus was on earth; we were constantly using every opportunity to bring him down. Since there was no substance to any negative thing we could expose about him, we had to change our tactics. We had to move from objective facts to subjective feelings. Such unsubstantiated squishy, intangible things like: character, credentials, motive, and mission are all marvelous ways to put a would-be leader in a negative light. These kind of feelings do not even need to be proven but can do major damage in disenchanting a would-be audience. Remember that most people will not invest the time or energy in a fact-finding mission but will cling to their misconceived first impression. Remember that is how we repeatedly attacked the Enemy when he was on earth. Even though his trial and execution was unjustified, it was after all by public ascent the he was crucified. The majority won…and we helped! Damon, never minimize what you can accomplish with a misdirected crowd or misguided few.

This leads me to your current work with Claudia. Faithful people like her who live consistent lives in public and private are so dangerous but thankfully so few! You have done what you must to get rumors started that question everything from her character to her motives. These questions must be the kind that can only be felt, even if they cannot be proven in any substantive way. If you work hard enough on ruining how people perceive her, you help facilitate questions about the credibility of her work and make her spend an extraordinary amount of well-wasted time coming to her own defense. For every moment she has to spend defending herself, you rob her of opportunities to do positive work for the Enemy.

Never let the Enemy's people consider long the silence of Jesus before those accusers on earth and at the end of time, as Daniel predicted, before the Antichrist. Help them to mistake such silence before his accusers as weakness or ever an admission of guilt. Never let them see such silence as a refusal to accept the notion that perception is truth, or that truth will ultimately be its own defense. You have been helpful, Damon, in getting all kinds of perception issues and

LETTER THIRTEEN - PERCEPTION IS TRUTH...ISN'T IT?

consequent rumors stirred up about Claudia. Keep that going! Claudia's relationship with Mark is great fodder for such hypercritical whisperings, as she naively reaches out to him in his time of need. You have done a great job in nurturing all the behind-the-scenes discussion about this relationship as to "who knows what else might be going on, especially in light of Mark's lurid past and Claudia's contrasting innocence." Keep stirring up that pot and adding fuel to that fire! Claudia, as you know, has also been given a new position of leadership in the church. She has been elected the first woman president of Church in the Valley Council. This in and of itself has caused some "big" discussion, providing as usual, much more fire than light. Combining this with her more visible involvement in Sunday morning worship makes her a great target. You have done right by encouraging those who are envious and confused, to challenge her on everything from her credentials to lead, to her motives for being front and center in worship. You must find what her weakest spots of criticism are such as integrity and motive and push as hard as you can. Unfortunately this Claudia does not see her lack of defense as weakness because she is just imitating the Enemy when he found himself in such a similar firing line.

Remember that if burned at the stake of public opinion, one such as this can be more dangerous to us when she is gone, than in her seemingly defenseless presence here. For some reason, today's wrong perceptions will fall away like chaff to wheat in time and reveal the real truth that was there all along. So whatever you do try to make her say or do something in defensive desperation, so that people can either try to dismiss her credibility now or in the future. Unfortunately with this one, it will be hard to do, as she is so absorbed with defending the Enemy in a cruel world that she probably will find little time or impetus to come to her own defense.

Oh, I am so over this Claudia! Be thankful, Damon, that her kind is so very rare. We have wasted too much time and energy on her. She disgusts me with her understanding of our power and of course the Enemy's vigilant presence. Worst yet she knows of her own weakness and dependence solely on him. She has that complete surrender and child-like trust that the Enemy is her mighty fortress and foundation…in good times and bad.

Damon, this rumor mongering may not work. So if you cannot get her to come to her own defense or rely on her own strength, at least turn critics to fans and make them just try to imitate and follow her. Whatever you do, do not encourage them to trust and follow the Enemy as she does.

That's my perception…and I'm sticking with it!

Your so very likable and electable,

Uncle Scratch

LETTER FOURTEEN
LOVE: AGAINST SUCH THERE IS NO LAW

"Damon the whole reason for this Inquisition Conference for you stems from *that* worship service that took place here three weeks ago! It was absolutely unacceptable! We must double up our efforts to somehow get these folks' focus off of the Enemy. It was bad enough to have Claudia so genuinely connected to the Enemy, but now there seem to be so many like her. It is really disgusting to see this crowd really meaning what they are saying and living out their faith. What is most painful are the many new ones who are signing up to fight with the Enemy. Damon, how did this happen on your watch? I warned you how dangerous this could be. My note to you a couple weeks ago about *that* worship experience still burns me up! I told you specifically to do anything to keep their faith and life as separate as possible and certainly not genuine or real. Remember in my letter to you on this I quoted myself from our manual:

> "If people prayed as much as they talked about prayer and prayed *for* people as much as they talked *about* people, we would find ourselves in a most unfortunate way."

Dear Damon,

I am afraid that you are getting soft on me. I heard about last Sunday's worship at Church in the Valley. There has never been a time when I was this concerned about anything this destructive to our cause at this church. This past Sunday certainly was different. I should have known when Pastor Tim stood up in front of the congregation and rattled off his familiar sermon opener, "Let the words of my mouth and the meditations of my heart be acceptable in your sight, O Lord," that we were in for a *long* service! It was the first time, in my memory, that he actually sincerely spoke these words directly to the Enemy.

That should have been a clue as to what was about to come. It was a time in which these folks didn't just mouth confession but experienced it firsthand. How could you let that happen, and in the context of Sunday worship? Damon, how this happened is beyond me!

The pastor invited two people to come forward —no I guess it was three. Mark, whose year-old conversion and battle with drugs and all kinds of addictions has been legendary news at Church in the Valley. Then there was Pastor Brian, whose affair with one of the church secretaries has been well documented and discussed at length. Last of all was Pastor Tim's wife, Maggie. She was brought forward in a wheelchair in the midst of a horrific battle with terminal cancer. Beginning with Mark, Pastor Tim invited each to speak.

LETTER FOURTEEN - LOVE: AGAINST SUCH THERE IS NO LAW

Damon, then things went from bad to worse! Mark shared, with tears I might add, that he had been battling with his drug and alcohol addictions. He had been found by God at Church in the Valley and helped by all but particularly by his dear friend Claudia, which made a few rumor mongers squirm. He said that he was winning the battle with the Enemy's help. He thanked the church for all the support and love, and he went on to say that he had been lying to himself and everyone. Then with a quick smile, "If any of you have missed me, I have been gone the past six weeks getting help." He shared that he had been at rehab again for the past six weeks. He revealed that he was not finished, but in process. And concluded, "I hope that the people of the Church in the Valley will have me back and continue to help and pray for me." There was total silence and I thought the lizard like, beady eyes of those in the front pews were some sign of the fiery blaze of judgment to come. But no…of all people Mr. Lundgren, Oscar that is, broke the silence even without a nod of assent from his doting wife, Ginger. That trouble maker, who I could always count on to inject a bit of chaos, stood up with tears streaming down his face and began to applaud. Within seconds every member was applauding with affirmation of Mark.

Damon, it does not get much worse than that! Steam is shooting out of my horns just recalling this! No one needed to pray or read any scriptures—they lived it out, which is our worst nightmare! Afterward Mark was hugged by half the church, which by the way, is a something new for Church in the Valley and something we must attempt to kill ASAP. The next person to stand was Pastor Brian and things continued to unravel!

Pastor Brian stood up with his wife, Sharon. I knew everyone was expecting his resignation as we had helped to stimulate plenty of conversation about that beforehand. It was logical to think, in light of his affair with one of the church secretaries, that he would step down. Damon, I know you had done all you could to keep those rumors alive and fanned the flames of the affair as much as possible, too. Instead of him speaking, he introduced, in very loving terms, his wife, Sharon. She then stood up and spoke. She spoke with such clarity and sincere eloquence that her words were secondary to her stellar presence, something I have seldom witnessed in Church in the Valley before.

She said that she, as well as everyone else, was quite aware of her husband's infidelity. She shared that she had spoken with Tiffany, the church secretary, and more importantly had confronted Brian. She said that she and her husband began to pray together and for the first time in their ministry, truly understood that the church was a mission and ministry but also was a living, dynamic organism. Because of that, she said, it was also very fragile and sensitive, and that when one part hurts, every part hurts; when one part is unfaithful, all parts suffer.

Brian stood up and apologized to the church for any and all hurt he had inflicted on his family and his church family. He went on to ask for a fresh start with the church as his wife had given him. He indicated that he and Sharon would continue going to counseling and if they would keep him on, he would work with Pastor Tim and the church for a six-month probation period. Before he could go further, good old Oscar, who was on a radically uncharacteristic mission of forgiveness, stood and led the congregation in another symbolic acceptance of Pastor Brian and Sharon.

LETTER FOURTEEN - LOVE: AGAINST SUCH THERE IS NO LAW

Damon, the worst of possibilities happened in that hour, which seemed like days. No one, it seems, was outside the realm of the Enemy's redemption. That word is harmless by itself, but when it is experienced, it is lethal. Remember we are supposed to do our best to stifle that experience at all costs, and particularly, in churches!

The whole mess climaxed when Pastor Tim wheeled his wife into the center aisle. He kissed her head, wiped her eyes, which had been overtaken with the kind of emotion sweeping over everyone in that place. He then went behind the altar, took the flowers from there, and put them in her lap. He smiled, she cried more, and he spoke of their thirty-one years of marriage. He shared that, as everyone probably knew, his wife, Maggie, had been diagnosed with terminal pancreatic cancer and sixteen months earlier had been given six months to live. He went on to say that his love for his wife had never diminished, but his time with her certainly would. Fighting back tears, he said that he would like to be at home, by her side in the last days, which would mean in the ensuing months that, "I will be at home instead of here, if it is okay with you." Then there came a very visible wink, nod of approval, and tears from Pastor Tim's nemesis, Oscar Lundgren. Damon, what in heaven's name was with that old Oscar Lundgren...too much Starbucks' that morning?

What followed really got me steamed. For years Damon, we have tried to make the cross and the Enemy's sacrifice a horrific and nonsensical event that he had to dutifully suffer on behalf of his wayward children. Our emphasis has been to lift up the *have to* nature of this, as if the Enemy is a reluctant parent, dreadfully cleaning up the kid's mess. Damon, we abhor *any* reference to the cross, but at the very least, we can distort its meaning. Make it a symbol of a necessary, but painfully reluctant, laborious sacrifice rather than a real, tender act of compassion. I bring all this up precisely because Pastor Tim did what we so try to avoid. He used an example of the relationship with his wife to demonstrate the Enemy's relationship with them.

He then took the cross from the altar, set it beside his wife and her wheelchair, and said, "Up until now I have never before understood Jesus' Words, 'I am the Good Shepherd; The Good Shepherd lays down His life for His sheep, no one takes it from Him but He gives it of His own accord.'"

He then went on to say that people have asked him about caring for his wife and how difficult that must be. He said, "I realize it will be challenging, and the doctor has told us it will be." He said, "Maggie will get to the point that she will not recognize me, and I will be rushing home to tend to her, changing her clothes at the most inopportune times." Then as he wrapped his arms around his seated wife he said, "There is no one else in the world who I would want to do this, because no one in the world can love Maggie with the kind of love that I have for her." He said, "I have finally understood what Jesus meant when he said that he gave his life and love of his own will and desire for us. You see no one could love us like he could, and he would not want anyone else to do it for us. He didn't go to the cross begrudgingly any more than I will face each day begrudgingly. There is no one I love more or could care for more…than my Maggie. It is my honor and my joy to be by her side…always, and particularly now." The pastor then literally crumbled with

LETTER FOURTEEN - LOVE: AGAINST SUCH THERE IS NO LAW

emotion and slowly pulled himself back up, grabbing the altar cross, and going on to say as he held it up, "That is what the cross is all about. In these past twelve years of ministry at Church in the Valley, I hope that you have been able to experience that cross-shaped love…firsthand." He leaned over and kissed his wife with a passionate kiss of a newlywed; that was followed by more *&@+ applause and the passing of the peace. Damon, it doesn't get any worse than this! I think you actually had a twinge of, what shall I say… emotion? I am deeply concerned about your commitment to our cause. Since I cannot fire you, I will fire you up…trust me! I will also see that you are removed from this district and that you have some time off to re-ignite your mission of chaos and deceit.

Your disappointed but ever vigilant,
Uncle Scratch

"Damon that letter is still hot off the press. The service was just several weeks ago. It is time for us to leave and get to work! There is so much work to do and such an unsuspecting world out there.

"I hope that my sharing these letters with you has inspired you to use all the tricks we have! By the way, even after *that* service, you forgot a real trick of our trade—never underestimate the potential of the church parking lot following a service. Remember a few seconds of angry exchanges from impatient "Christian" drivers can ruin hours of the best worship experiences. You must *always* be thinking about how you can turn something *good* into something *bad*.

"Do your best, I mean worst…I'll be watching!"

MEET THE FAMILY / SATAN UNDERCOVER
Small group/self-study questions

Read: Ezekiel 28:12-19
What does this tell us about Satan?
Was he co-equal with God? Martin Luther once said that, "Satan is God's lackey."
What does this mean? Was he given everything from God?

Read: Isaiah 14:12-17
Read over the five "I Wills" of Satan
Do we also assert our own will against God? How?
Discuss the two Gardens—Eden and Gethsemane (view the opening of the movie, *The Passion of Christ*– garden scene)
What are the differences between *my will* and *thy will*?

Does it make a difference in our lives if we know that there is a third party influence like Satan tempting us in our choices and decisions?
Would we see activities like worship, Bible study, and prayer differently?

Do you agree that we probably need to be reminded to see this life as both a battlefield on which to engage, as well as a playground to enjoy?

What does this mean for how our families, children, grandchildren, and loved ones see life?

Read: Ephesians 6:10-18

Do you think that we truly could benefit from awareness of Satan's schemes and deceit in our lives and in the world?

If we understood Old Scratch and his ways, would this make us eager to learn more about how God intends for us to take on the full armor he offers?

A LONE VOICE IN THE WILDERNESS OF NOISE
Small group/self-study questions

Music: "Word of God Speak" Mercy Me

Do you think we need more quiet time and places to ask for guidance and to listen for God?

Read: Matthew 13:11-17
Jesus often used these words, "Eyes to see and to ears to hear."
What might keep us from seeing or hearing what God is telling us or leading us to do?
Does noise and busyness sometimes serve as real distractions?
Contrast this with 1 Corinthians 2:9 "How might we miss what God has in store for us?"

"The sole cause of man's unhappiness is that he does not know how to stay quietly in his room. What people want is not the easy peaceful life that allows us to think of our unhappy condition. That is why we prefer the hunt to the capture. That is why we choose some attractive object to entice us in ardent pursuit." –Blaise Pascal 1

Is it easy to equate our noise from TVs, cell phones, and radios and our every-minute busyness to doing God's work? How might this be Satan's tool as well?

Read: Luke 10:38-42

Mary and Martha are both doing "good" things. What is it that Jesus said Mary had chosen?
Why did he describe it that way?
Has there been a time in your life when Jesus has particularly and powerfully revealed Himself to you in a quiet time, retreat, or word of scripture?

Read: John 10:10

What does Jesus mean by *abundant life*?
Do you think Christians should be the most joyful of all people?
Holiness: "Little people think that Holiness is dull. When one meets the real thing it is irresistible." –C.S. Lewis 2
How would you say that quote describes Claudia?
How does she embody true holiness?
Does this statement sound appropriate for her? "Live your life in such a way that when your feet hit the floor in the morning, Satan shudders and says, 'Oh shoot, she's awake!'"
What makes her so appealing and special?

Would you agree with Martin Luther that all God's commands truly fall under the first commandment?

How does Claudia deal with all the cultural idolatries and entrapments of the world?

What are some things that might become a god to us in our culture, in our lives?

Read: Romans 12:1

It is interesting that Paul uses imagery of a living sacrifice. As a living sacrifice, what might we decide to do "when placed on the altar?"

Is there a need to commit and recommit to God as living sacrifices daily? Always?

Is Christianity in essence giving up and surrendering before we have to?

Does this have anything to do with taking up our crosses—daily?

1. Blaise Pascal , "*Pensees*," pp 37-39
2. C.S Lewis, "*A Letter to an American Lady*," pg. 19

LAW AND GOSPEL
Small group/self-study questions

Poem "Given for All"
A tender loving Father
Gifts His Children with food
For the arduous journey of life
Food, none other than…
Himself
rather than graciously gobbling it up along the way,
Like manna
They stop and ponder
Hoarding and
Drawing lines,
Where there are none,
Issuing childish edicts
About taking
As to who, when, why, and with whom,
Forgetting that He said…
"Take and eat"
Not..
Take and understand, take and confine, take and redefine

But "take and eat"
Being never ready, never worthy; always grateful
It will never be more simple,
nor more profound
Than that
And only a GIFT,
when taken as such.

Music: "Love Them Like Jesus" Casting Crowns

Read: Matthew 9:9-13

What was Matthew considered by the people of his day?

How did Jesus interact with him?

Was Jesus the perfect balance of Law and Gospel? How?

Who probably gathered for Matthew's party after his calling?

How did the religious leaders respond to Jesus' calling of Matthew?

In your church and in your understanding of church, who is welcome to worship?

Who is welcome to join? Have you ever been excluded?

Who is welcome to receive Holy Communion or to be baptized?

How do these answers reflect your understanding of God's grace—his Law and his Gospel?

How do you think Jesus would answer these questions?

Read: Ephesians 4:15

"Speaking the truth in love" sounds like Law and Gospel. Describe.

Do you think to simply lift up one of these polarities of truth or love at the exclusion of the other can be harmful?

Is the example of parenting a good one, using both Law and Gospel, and truth and love?

Do you know of any example of a church or family who went through the experience of one at the exclusion of the other? What were the results?

Would you describe *tough love* as Law or Gospel? Or would you describe it as Law and Gospel?

Have you ever known anyone who used *tough love* in real life relationships/situations?

SEARCH FOR CONSENSUS: A MORAL MAJORITY?
Small group/self-study questions

Rabbi Finklestein was meeting with his board. He was certain that the synagogue was to have a building program and knew that the board would be totally opposed to this idea. He still presented the idea and was handily voted down twelve to one. So the good rabbi said, "Let us pray and ask for divine direction." As the rabbi prayed, there was thunder and lightning, and the board members were knocked off their feet. There was fire and smoke as the large table that they were around broke in two. The rabbi stood up untouched and said, "Well I guess we have heard!" The president of the board stood up, badly shaken, and as he brushed the dust off his coat and straightened his badly bent glasses, said, "Not so fast. It is still just twelve to two on this vote!"
— Isaac Asimov

Read: Romans 3:23

What does Paul mean by *all*?
What is it that we have fallen short of?

In your earlier look at the two gardens, Eden and Gethsemane; contrast Adam's and Jesus' attitudes and actions.

How powerful is self-will?
What did C.S. Lewis mean in the *Problem of Pain* when he said, "The doors of hell are locked from the inside?"
"I Did It My Way," is a song made popular by Frank Sinatra.
How much importance is put on doing things our way and on our self-determination?

Toward the end of his life, English King Henry VIII wore a gold bracelet that read *tot morir que changes ma pensee* (to die rather than change my mind).
How important is it to say that we follow God's direction in our decisions and choices?

Majority Rule:
During the statesman de Toqueville's visit to young America, he expressed concerns about majority rule, thinking it might be devoid of justice or morality.
How does that relate to this chapter and the desire to follow God's lead and voice as opposed to the world's direction?
Do you think that there is danger in a democracy that is devoid of morality or absolute values?
Could the majority truly become its own morality?
Could the majority consensus become the new rule of law outside any reference to God or the scriptures?
Do you see this happening today?

Discuss C.S. Lewis's comment that "the real reason for democracy is that man is so fallen that no man can ever be trusted with unchecked power over his fellows." 1

How do we find directions from God when it comes to our decisions and actions?

What role do the scriptures, other Christians, prayer, and circumstances play in our decision-making process?

What role does the majority opinion play in our life decision and choices?

1. C.S Lewis, *"Present Concerns,"* pg 17

SEX AND THE MARKETPLACE
Small group/self-study questions

Music: "Stay Strong" Newsboys

Read: Romans 1:21-25

What does this tell you about the problem of sexuality as it has been misused and disconnected from God's original intentions?
Has this always been a problem for the human race?

C.S. Lewis called badness/sin "spoiled goodness." 1
How might our sexuality when wrongly used be spoiled goodness?
Do you agree that Satan probably relishes those moments when we take God-given gifts that he intended for good and turn them into dirty and bad things?
What are some recent examples?

Do you think that as Christians who personally know the Designer and Creator of our sexuality that we should be unapologetically able to enjoy the intimacy he intended for us?

Is there a dichotomy of poles in society, often mirrored by the church, that lifts up the extremes of either the "*Victorian*" no or the "*Playboy*" yes when it comes to sexuality?

Do you think that there needs to be a balance which respects the power and potential of sexuality on the one hand and on the other hand enjoys the beautiful gift in the way God intended us to enjoy it?

Do you agree that this problem of misused sexuality is more pronounced in society today than before?

What role does advanced communication/media play?

Do you think it is a tool Satan uses to bring down leaders and to disenchant and disengage followers too?

Does the marketplace mentality of I want, therefore I get have a real part in infidelity?

Have you ever heard one who has been involved in extramarital affairs refer to their situation as necessary for "my happiness," "my need," or "my right"?

Have you ever noticed such justification ever to be cloaked in religious language that God intended this?

Is it strange how we misuse and abuse by "demonizing" and making unspiritual and foreign something as natural and real as our sexuality?

Why do you think this is?

Do you think there is an active third party who desires to "spoil" the good God intended for us?

Does the awareness and recognition of this help us to better face temptations in our lives in the world?

1. C.S Lewis, "*Mere Christianity,.*" pg. 314

CREATING CHAOS: DIVISIONS IN THE CHURCH
Small group/self-study questions

"This life therefore is not righteousness, but growth in righteousness, not health but healing, not being but becoming, not rest but exercise. We are not yet what we shall be, but we are growing toward it. The process is not yet finished but is going on, this is not the end but it is the road. All does not gleam in glory but all is being purified."
–Martin Luther 1

Read: 1 Corinthians 12:14-30

What does it mean to know that the church is the body of Christ?
Is one part more important than another?
Would you agree that all of us are equal in importance?
Who is at the head of the body?
How significant is it to realize this in all the roles we play?
How might such an emphasis curtail the kind of conflict that Pastor Tim and Mr. Lundgren are having?

Do you know of any churches/congregations in conflict? Without revealing names, what are some of the details?

What role would selfish and self-serving, agendas play in these conflicts?

Augustine and Luther referred to this as *in curvatus se*—a turning in on oneself. Explain.

Do you think that some conflicts are inevitable in families and church families?

Is it important how we handle these?

What difference does it make if we know that Christ is the head?

What difference does it make to know that there may be a third party (Old Scratch) engaged and interested in stirring up the pot?

Read: John 17:20-25

What was Jesus' desire for us?

The Trinity has been referred to as the perfect dance or perichoresis. Instead of a triangle, the Trinity is best symbolized as a dynamic moving circle. The Father points away from himself, to the Son, the Son, to the Holy Spirit, and then back to the Father. It is a constant motion of love, which constantly lifts up the other—three in one.

How does this relate to our lives together, particularly as you read Philippians 2:1-5?

Do you agree that being one in unity as the body is not something we need to create on our own for we need only to truly and fully live in him?

How might humility before the head, Christ Jesus, and one another help in conflict resolution?

Does taking time away, as modeled by Jesus and needed by the pastor, lift up the need for inspired directions and strength other than our own?

Can God use conflict to help us repent and surrender to him?

The Jewish Talmud has a marvelous thought: "God's spirit surrounds a hardened heart so that when it finally cracks the spirit can seep in."

Considering the quote from Luther, how does it help to humbly admit that in this life we are in on a journey and in a process rather than at our destination and in possession of all the answers?

Ruth Graham once pointed to a sign she saw after traveling through some road construction with her husband, Billy. "I want that word on my gravestone," she said. The sign read End of Construction; Thanks for Your Patience."

How disarming is it when we candidly admit our need for forgiveness and our dependence on Christ as the head?

How might this potentially help to squelch and redirect conflicts?

1. Martin Luther, *"Defense and Explanation of all the Articles : Second Article,"* (1521)

THE END: RAPTURE—GOING OR STAYING
Small group/self-study questions

Music: "We Are Not Home Yet" Steven Curtis Chapman
"On the Willows" Godspell
"Another Time, Another Place" Sandy Patti

Read: Matthew 24:36-44

Only the Father knows the exact details of the end of time—not Jesus while on earth or the angels or Satan. What does this mean to you?

Is it good to trust God for these details?

Should we live each day as if in the end times?

C.S. Lewis put it this way, "Aim at heaven and you will get earth thrown in. Aim at earth and you will get nothing." Lewis also noted, "If you read history, you will find that the Christians who did most in the present world were precisely those who taught most of the next. It is since Christians have largely ceased to think of the other world that they have become so ineffective in this one." 1

Do you agree that considering this life and this world as "foreign" land helps us engage more meaningfully here in the life and world?

Have you ever had the response of a loved one on their deathbed, speak of going home—meaning their heavenly home?

Perhaps he or she even spoke about loved ones who had preceded him or her in death. Was this helpful and comforting? Explain.

As Christians, how can we keep the balance between this world of being content and appreciative of all that we have here and at the same time not be entrapped, enticed, and consumed by all that it has to offer?

How does Satan win if we are convinced that it doesn't get any better than this life/world? Or, that it has never been better than this?

Read: Romans 8:22-25

All of creation mourns for a lost good.
What was Eden like?
Is being in perfect relationship with God purely natural?

"Grace is rather the power of God revealed in Christ which destroys the unnatural, destroys man's refusal to be natural. Grace thus makes nature what it was intended to be. In that sense grace perfects nature—not because it adds what was lacking, but precisely because it makes nature to be nature once again. The grace of God is power strong enough to make and keep us human."–Gerhard Forde **2**

Is it possible that realities like *death* and *evil* seem unnatural or foreign to us because we have a distant memory that mourns for this lost good of Eden, where death and evil did not exist?

Should our distant memory of the perfect past and our anticipation of the future heaven help us live *rootless* in the present?

Is earth a foreign land?

Do you think that we are not home yet?

How else might we live like we are not home yet?

1. C.S. Lewis, "*Mere Christianity,*" pg 134
2. Gerhard Forde, "*Where God Meets Man,*" pp 56, 57

COUNT IT ALL…WHAT?
Small group/self-study questions

Claudia's poem after 9/11
"Eyes Wide Open"

The winter of our souls
whose unwelcome intrusion does come to all,
respecting neither season, nor person, nor time,
disturbs and disrupts us all…blowing
It's icy uninvited chill
Wherever and upon whomever it will

Such an uninvited intruder as this…
However greeted…
determines our true fate.
If as an unnamed, unidentifiable stranger;
We turn away with angry fist and closed eyes…
Leaving us empty and flattened.
Hollowed and void of all spirit within
But if these harsh unwelcome storms are
faced, though never fully understood,
braced for, in whatever does come,

on bended knee with squinted but open lids;
riveted to an unseen Benevolent hand.

When struggles cease and dust does settle
From the charred remains around
will rise…
inspired, refined, distilled
the vestige remains of what will have become.
A new creation

Music: "Praise You in This Storm" Casting Crowns

Read: James 1:2-3

How does James say we should take trouble and trials?
What do you think he means when he says "count it all joy *when* not *if* trials come?
Is it dangerous for us to assume that our faith in God will guarantee good circumstances?
What role do feelings really play in our belief and trust in God?

Would you agree that some Christians who have faced the most difficult of circumstances and yet continued faithful have a powerful witness and testimony?
What does this say about them and about God?

Mother Teresa's diary was recently recovered from her time in India. The diary was filled with heartache and doubts, and some in the media viewed it as an example of her faltering faith.

Do you think it is okay sometimes to have our doubts about God?

Is God big enough to handle these doubts?

Mother Teresa was once asked how she could do ministry in the squalor of the poor and dying in India. Her response was that she "could not do it without her faith in God."

Read: Matthew 13:1-9/18-23 "The Parable of the Sower and the Seed"

Considering all these examples of the seed not taking root, what role would you say feelings play especially with regard to the trials and crucibles of life?

What might some of the different threats to the growth of seed represent regarding our faith?

Would you agree that whatever challenges—shallowness, sun, birds, rock—it is how we face these challenges that truly determines how our faith will be rooted and grow? Explain.

ANSWERED PRAYERS
Small group/self-study questions

Read: Daniel 9:4-19

What do you notice about Daniel's powerful prayer of intercession?

Do you agree that prayer may be the single most powerful force for change in the world?

How has your life been impacted by prayer? What about the lives of others?

What if it is true that God is a gentleman who gets involved only when *invited*?

How might prayer for one's self and others provide that open door/window to God?

Read: Matthew 6:9-15

Jesus introduced the terminology of *Father* or more literally *Abba-Daddy* when addressing God.

What do you think about that closeness?

Do our prayers reflect that kind of close and personal relationship?

Is it necessary for a child to be formal when addressing his or her dad?

What else does it mean to call God Father?

Read: Luke 18:1-5

Jesus teaches us to be persistent in prayer.

Do you think we ever pray with the kind of involvement and intensity for others and ourselves that we should?

Does it make sense that in prayer we surrender and empty ourselves to the very heart of God?

When we ask for God's will especially in a difficult situation involving life and death, is it possible that there might be more to God's answer than physical healing or than life versus death?

What is the *ultimate* healing from a Christian's viewpoint?

Often we do more talking about prayer than praying; take time alone or in your small group to pray.

WORSHIPING THEIR WORSHIP
Small group/self-study questions

Music: "The Heart of Worship (When the Music Fades)" Matt Redman

The Scottish catechism says, "That the Chief aim of humans is to Glorify God."
How true is this as a goal for our worship?
Do we sometimes miss the mark as to what truly brings glory to God?

In worship, how is God truly the audience?
What role do we have both in leading and participating in worship?

Read: II Samuel 6:1-11

David, in his innocent enthusiasm, rushed forward with the ark forgetting God's command and wishes.
How do you think we might be tempted to run "ahead of God" in our excitement?
Do we often put our plans ahead of God's? How?

Read: I Chronicles 21:1-8
       II Samuel 24:1-3

Once again, David does a seemingly innocent thing by taking a census.

What was wrong with that?

Are these examples of when our desire to be in control, go it alone, or get ahead of God can get us in trouble?

Discuss the balance of practical actions and trusting faith.

What part does a grateful satisfaction play in truly worshiping God?

Is it possible to get so focused on perfunctory details of worship that we miss focusing on who we are worshiping?

ANOTHER GIFT TO SPOIL— THE WORD
Small group/self-study questions

Music: "Thy Word" Amy Grant

Read: Colossians 3:16
Read: Psalm 119:97-106

How has God's Word been like a lamp to your feet to light your path?

What are some of your favorite most inspiring scriptures? Why?

Read: II Chronicles 7:14
Read: Deuteronomy 11:18-21

Is part of our turning to God also turning to his Word?

Do we sometimes need to be encouraged to get back to the Word?

Discuss Josiah's reform in the Old Testament.

Read: Isaiah 55:9-11

What is God's promise regarding his Word?
Has this been your experience?
Is there always a treasure to find when we dig in?
Is this treasure sometimes immediately realized and at other times, maybe months, years removed?
How does the fact that God chooses ordinary people and nations to use for His purposes make you feel?
Can you imagine if God's Word was not honest, relevant, and real to life?
Are there truly any perfect biblical heroes? Families? Societies?

What do you think Luther meant when he said that scriptures is a "Living Word"?
How has God's Word spoken to you in difficult and trying times?
Can we learn from other denominations when it comes to interpreting and understanding scripture?

PERCEPTION IS TRUTH… OR IS IT?
Small group/self-study questions

Read: Psalm 46

How is God your fortress and defense?
What does it mean to call God this particularly when we face difficulties and challenges?
Have you ever been slandered or misrepresented?
What is our first inclination to do?

Read: Deuteronomy 3:21-22
Read: II Chronicles 20:15

Who ultimately will defend and fight for us?
Who are we accountable to?

What was Jesus response to his accusers in Matthew 26:62-68?

What will his response be at the end of times as Son of Man with the ancient of days?

Read: Daniel 7:11-14

Contrast Christ's silence to the "boastful" words of the horn (Antichrist).
Does the truth ultimately need our verbal defense?

What do you think about G.K Chesterton's observation that, "when people stop believing in God, they don't believe in nothing; they believe in anything."

Is there a danger in not believing is an absolute truth?
Do you agree that in our culture perception is truth?
Do you think that we live in a culture that promotes that?

LOVE: AGAINST SUCH THERE IS NO LAW
Small group/self-study questions

Read: 1 Corinthians 13

Music – "Revelation Song" - Kari Jobe

This scripture is so commonly read in weddings.
What is Paul saying?
How does it relate to what precedes it at the end of chapter 12?

Read: Ephesians 3:14-21

The mission that the Apostle Paul shares is that "we may be filled to the measure of all the fullness of God."
What does that mean?
How did Church in the Valley experience that?

For individual sharing:
Share a time in your life through worship, retreat, conference, prayer, or Bible study, when the grace, forgiveness, and love of God came together in a powerful life-changing way for you.

Made in the USA
Charleston, SC
04 April 2010